"Let's play a little dodgeball!"

Each time a kid got hit, Coach yelled, "Out!" and pointed. The kid who got hit would have to sit on the bleachers. Phillip could hardly believe that kids with balls were purposely aiming at ones without them.

Whap! A boy standing near the line got it in the gut.

Whack! A girl who had turned to run got it in the back.

A ball zipped so close to Phillip, he could hear the air scream. The girl next to him twisted to avoid a low ball. She slipped, and the ball hit her as she lay on the ground. A circular red spot formed on her exposed back thigh before she staggered away.

Phillip had lost three-quarters of his team. Fewer kids meant more balls thrown his way. He caught a glimpse of the clock. Maybe he could survive until the bell. He backed himself in the far corner.

"Get the new kid," a familiar voice yelled. It was B.B. Tyson, the hall monitor. She lobbed a screamer right at him. It barely missed. There was no place to go.

OTHER BOOKS YOU MAY ENJOY

THE Stupendous
DODGEBALL
Fiasco

THE Stupendous DODGEBALL Fiasco

Janice Repka

PUFFIN BOOKS
An Imprint of Penguin Group (USA) Inc.

PUFFIN BOOKS
Published by the Penguin Group
Penguin Young Readers Group, 345 Hudson Street, New York, New York 10014, U.S.A.
Penguin Group (Canada), 90 Eglinton Avenue East, Suite 700, Toronto, Ontario, Canada M4P 2Y3
(a division of Pearson Penguin Canada Inc.)
Penguin Books Ltd, 80 Strand, London WC2R 0RL, England
Penguin Ireland, 25 St Stephen's Green, Dublin 2, Ireland (a division of Penguin Books Ltd)
Penguin Group (Australia), 250 Camberwell Road, Camberwell, Victoria 3124, Australia
(a division of Pearson Australia Group Pty Ltd)
Penguin Books India Pvt Ltd, 11 Community Centre,
Panchsheel Park, New Delhi - 110 017, India
Penguin Group (NZ), 67 Apollo Drive, Rosedale, Auckland 0632, New Zealand
(a division of Pearson New Zealand Ltd.)
Penguin Books (South Africa) (Pty) Ltd, 24 Sturdee Avenue,
Rosebank, Johannesburg 2196, South Africa

Registered Offices: Penguin Books Ltd, 80 Strand, London WC2R 0RL, England

First published in the United States of America by Dutton Children's Books,
a division of Penguin Young Readers Group, 2004
Published by Puffin Books, a division of Penguin Young Readers Group, 2012

1 3 5 7 9 10 8 6 4 2
Copyright © Janice Repka, 2004
Illustrations copyright © Glin Dibley, 2004

All rights reserved

THE LIBRARY OF CONGRESS HAS CATALOGED THE DUTTON CHILDREN'S BOOKS EDITION AS FOLLOWS:
Repka, Janice.
The stupendous dodgeball fiasco / by Janice Repka ; illustrated by Glin Dibley.
p. cm.
Summary: Eleven-year-old Phillip's dream of running away from the circus comes true
when his parents allow him to stay with relatives in Hardingtown, Pennsylvania, where
dodgeball is practically a religion and life is anything but normal.
ISBN: 0-525-47346-7 (hc)
[1. Ball games—Fiction. 2. Schools—Fiction. 3. Blind—Fiction.
4. People with disabilities—Fiction. 5. Moving, Household—Fiction.
6. Circus—Fiction. 7. Pennsylvania—Fiction.]
I. Dibley, Glin, ill. II. Title.
PZ7.R2957St 2004
[Fic]—dc22 2004001984

Puffin Books ISBN 978-0-14-242107-9

Printed in the United States of America

For my stupendous mom, Frances Repka

J.R.

For K.K., S.K., L.K., and D.K.

G.D.

THE Stupendous DODGEBALL Fiasco

You can't stuff more than six clowns into a telephone booth. Eleven-year-old Phillip Edward Stanislaw had seen his dad try. But each time, a giant shoe or rubber nose stuck out, and the door wouldn't shut. Why should today be any different?

"Welcome to the Windy Van Hooten Circus," the announcer shouted. "Let the show begin."

In the right ring, white-faced clowns, juggling rubber chickens, raced on unicycles. In the left ring, Helena's Marvelous Miniature Horses balanced on their hind legs in hula skirts. Thrilled *oooohs* and *ahhhhs* poured through the tent, interrupted by thunderous bursts of applause.

Phillip yawned. He rested his head against the handle of his pooper-scooper shovel. He was standing in the exit aisle between two bleachers. If one of Helena's horses had an "accident" during the show, it was his job to run into the ring, scoop up the mess, and dispose of it in a special trash can. That way, she wouldn't slip.

The blended smell of elephants and hot dogs made Phillip's stomach ache. To take his mind off it, he daydreamed about the birthday present his dad, Leo Laugh-a-

Lot, had placed on the kitchen table that morning. The box was three feet long and wrapped in leftover Christmas paper turned inside out.

It couldn't be new circus stilts, Phillip thought. They're too long. Juggling pins are too short. A megaphone is too wide. Acrobat gloves are too small. There were no holes in the box, so it couldn't be a new pet for an animal act. What else could it be? He stared at a muddy spot on the ground just under the right stand. A dirty ticket stub was squashed into it.

Suddenly, Phillip thought of something that almost made him drop his shovel. Once he had found a muddy baseball card underneath the stands. The player on the card was holding a long wooden bat, exactly the size of the box on his kitchen table. Was it possible that, for the first time, his parents were giving him a gift that wasn't circus-related?

If only I knew how to operate a bat, he thought. I hope it comes with instructions.

Since the circus never stayed in one town very long, Phillip had never been to a baseball game. Because his family chose not to own a television, he'd never even seen a game. All he knew about baseball was from the card and from a poem he had read called "Casey at the Bat." The poem was about a great baseball player who embarrassed himself by losing a big game. Phillip did not want to embarrass himself.

What I need, he thought, is to find a regular kid who can give me some tips.

Phillip scanned the crowded bleachers and spotted a boy wearing a New York Yankees baseball cap, just like the cap worn by the man on the card. The boy ate cotton candy and watched Freckles spray Jingles with a bottle of seltzer water.

Leo Laugh-a-Lot threw a bucket of confetti, and the boy laughed.

If the boy could stay after the show, maybe he could help. Phillip would have to get a message to him. He waved to get his attention, but the boy wouldn't take his eyes off the show.

The clowns rolled out an old-fashioned telephone booth. The phone rang and BoBo rushed in, climbed to the top, and pinned himself against the ceiling. It rang again and Freckles followed, pressing himself against BoBo. Each time it rang, another clown would enter. The acrobat clowns, Versa-Vice and Vice-Versa, piled in. Cuddles and Jingles compressed themselves in the middle, a mass of twisted elbows and knees. Finally, Phillip's dad squeezed in. He tried to yank shut the door, but his extra-large clown rump, complete with pink satin boxers, got stuck. The booth swayed, making the audience sway with it.

Whap! It tipped over. Clowns scampered out, bowing and curtsying to the cheers.

Phillip searched the bleachers. Where was the boy? People, shaking with laughter, blocked his view. He dropped his shovel, climbed onto the bleachers, and awkwardly made his way through. Three times he had to apologize for stepping on toes. Finally, he made it to where he had seen the boy.

"Where is he?" Phillip asked a girl with braided hair. "The boy who was sitting next to you."

"What boy?" She eyed Phillip like he was an alien.

He wondered if the boy had been part of his daydream.

"Sit down," said a woman from behind him. "I'm trying to watch the horses."

The horses! He had forgotten. Phillip glanced into the left ring. Helena held a hoop, and Wonder Star jumped through. Behind them, a brown blob steamed. A couple hundred children were between Phillip and his shovel.

"I'm sorry. Pardon me. Coming through, please," he said, shuffling over peanut shells and empty cups. He bumped a man whose lemonade splashed down Phillip's shirt. Startled by the sudden cold drizzle, Phillip backed into a freckle-faced girl with a caramel apple.

Smack! The gooey ball hit him in the head and stuck to his hair.

"Gimme back my apple," the girl demanded. She grabbed the stick and pulled.

"*Ahhhhhhh!*" Phillip cried.

The girl tried to twirl the apple out, but this only made it stick more.

"Give her back her apple," said a teenage boy holding a bag of popcorn. Phillip darted out of the way as the teen lunged for him. The popcorn flew in the air and became rain. The kernels stuck to the gooey caramel.

In the left ring, Helena walked backward as Wonder Star led a dance line, each horse's front legs balanced on the horse before it. All were unaware of the slippery land mine ahead.

Squish!

Helena's foot hit the blob and skidded out from under her.

Fump!

She landed on her tush.

Her arms flailed back into a pile of hoops, sending them flying. Wonder

Star swerved and knocked over a rolling shelf loaded with props. The horses scattered as the props clattered to the ground.

The sounds of "Stars and Stripes Forever" filled the circus tent. Half the clowns chased after the horses, while the other half ran over to Helena.

"Ladies and gentlemen," the circus announcer shouted. "Please look to the skies for the death-defying Angela the Amazing Acrobat."

While the crowd diverted its attention to the high-wire act, Cuddles and Jingles helped Helena stand. Leo sprayed her backside clean with seltzer water. She looked like a stuffed doll limp from too many washings.

Phillip scurried to the edge of the bleachers. He fell and did a belly flop onto the ground. Peering up, he saw Helena leading Wonder Star out of the ring. She headed straight for him. He darted under the bleachers. The smell from Helena's boots made him pinch his nose to keep from gagging.

At least she doesn't see me, he thought.

Something pulled his hair.

"Ouch!" he cried.

Wonder Star yanked out a hunk of the gooey caramel apple.

"You!" Helena pulled Phillip by his ear. The horse balanced on her hind legs, begging for another bite.

"I'm out there slipping in poop, and you're taking a nap?" she snapped.

"I wasn't taking a nap," Phillip said, trying to escape from Wonder Star's appetite. Each time he moved, the horse moved, too. It looked like they were dancing. Helena grabbed Wonder Star by the bridle.

"Why were you hiding under the stands?" she demanded.

"I wasn't *under* the stands," Phillip said. "I was *in* them."

"In them? During the show?"

Phillip wanted to explain about his new bat and the boy in the baseball cap, but he doubted she would care. Helena wrested a piece of caramel apple stick from Wonder Star's mouth.

"You're a circus boy," she reminded Phillip. "You don't belong in the stands with the regular folks."

Phillip's eyes stung. He pulled up his T-shirt and rubbed his sweaty face. A piece of popcorn stuck to the lemonade stain scratched his cheek.

"Your mother will hear about this," Helena said. "Now go clean up that mess."

Phillip grabbed his shovel and raced out to the left ring. Why did things always go wrong for him?

Tiffany the Bearded Lady once told him that kids from the regular world dreamed of running away to join the circus. As he scooped away the afternoon's humiliation, Phillip wondered if he was the first kid who dreamed of running away from it.

One way to get elephant skin soft is to use furniture soap. But no matter how much furniture soap you use, an elephant will never be a coffee table.

As he hosed down Einstein the elephant after the show, Phillip thought: No matter how long I live with the circus, I'll never be a circus boy. "I'm tired of going to sleep in Silver City and waking up in Albuquerque," he confided to Einstein. "I hate not having friends my age. It's not fair. I want to live in a regular town, like a regular kid."

Einstein lifted a back leg and Phillip squirted his underside.

"Know what's the worst about circus life?"

The elephant flapped his huge ears.

"The way the audience looks at us. Mom and Dad don't even care. They want people to stare and laugh at them."

Einstein raised his trunk for a drink, and Phillip squirted into his mouth.

"Being in the circus makes you different," said Phillip. "Being different makes you a freak. That's not the life for me."

The side window to his family's trailer opened, and

Phillip saw Helena prop it with a piece of wood. Familiar voices drifted out. Phillip crept to the window to hear better.

"His heart's not in it," sighed Phillip's mother, Matilda the Fat Lady.

"That's no excuse," said Helena. "I can't do my act if I have to worry about slipping. He must pay attention. My Oscar could do it when he was Phillip's age."

"Well, if Oscar can do it . . ."

"Don't be ridiculous," said Helena. "You know Oscar gets shot from the cannon at three o'clock. He's busy preparing for that."

"Oscar could do it if we shot him out with the shovel in his hand," said Phillip's dad. He hit a button on his neck strap and his bow tie spun.

"Leo, it's time you stopped clowning and took matters seriously," Helena said. "Your son is not pulling his weight. He daydreams through his chores. He'd rather read a book than stick his head in a lion's mouth. He's doing crossword puzzles when he's supposed to be practicing his juggling. His behavior is most . . . uncircuslike."

"We'll talk to him," said Matilda.

"See that you do," said Helena. On her way out, she slammed the door to the trailer so hard it shook. Phillip hid behind Einstein until Helena was gone and then inched back to the window.

"Do you think buying him a baby chimpanzee would help?" Leo asked Matilda.

"We tried a pet," Matilda answered. "Remember the python disaster?"

"I still don't understand how that snake thought it could eat him."

"We've tried it all," she said. "Juggling lessons, the junior tuxedo and top hat, training stilts, the purple unicycle."

"He was crazy about that unicycle."

"He hated it."

"Well, he rode it like the wind."

"That's because you clowns chased after him, throwing custard pies."

"We were teaching him how to clown. He loved it."

"Is that why he fled up the rope to the trapeze artists' platform and hid from you?"

"He's a great climber," Leo said. "He could be an acrobat—if he didn't freeze at the top."

Matilda took her husband's thin, gloved hand and held it to her chubby cheek. "He's unhappy here," she said. "All he wants, all he's ever wanted, is to be a regular boy."

"But he's not a regular boy. He's a Stupendous Stanislaw."

"Maybe he wasn't meant for circus life," Matilda said.

"Nonsense," said Leo.

"We've discussed this so often," said Matilda. "Maybe it's time we let him make his own decision about what he wants to do. Send him to stay with my sister in Hardingtown. Let him get away from the circus for a while and experience what it's like to be in the real world."

Leo pulled off his floppy shoes and replaced them with his bunny slippers. "Children don't run away from the circus. He needs to find a way to fit in. Maybe if we sent him to clown school."

Outside, Phillip dropped the hose. It slithered back and forth, splashing his pants. Clown school! A room full of smelly makeup, tiny tricycles, and whipped-cream pies filled his head. He squeezed off the valve to the hose.

"Talk to him," Matilda said. "We have to do something."

"I'll talk to him," agreed Leo.

Phillip heard the trailer's squeaky door. He poured lemon-scented furniture soap onto Einstein's hide and began scrubbing with a long push broom.

"Whoa, boy," Leo said. "You don't want to wear a hole in him."

"I'm sorry," Phillip said. "I know I shouldn't have gone into the stands during the show." He gnawed his bottom lip. "Please don't make me do it, Dad."

"Do what?"

"Don't make me go to clown school. I'd make a terrible clown. I don't even have a sense of humor."

His dad laughed so hard he had to pinch his nose and hold his breath to regain his composure. Phillip hated how hard it was to have a serious conversation with a clown.

"Why were you in the stands?" Leo finally asked.

"I wanted to talk to a boy," Phillip said. "I should have waited. It won't happen again."

Einstein roared. Leo helped Phillip rinse him off. When they were done, they flipped their buckets and sat.

"What's it like, Dad? Life outside the circus?"

"Not as good."

"It's got to be better than shoveling elephant pens."

"Trust me, son."

"How will I ever know for sure?" Phillip asked.

"You belong here. You need to find something you're good at, that's all, and I have just the thing." Leo went into the trailer and came back with the long box. Matilda came out, too.

"Happy eleventh birthday, son," said Leo.

Phillip grabbed the present and tore into the wrapping paper. He lifted the top off the box and pushed aside the tissue. A long sword shone up at him.

"It's a swallowing sword," Leo said.

Phillip gulped.

"For a sword-swallowing act," Leo added.

Phillip stared at the shiny metal. He picked it up by the handle and watched the sun glint off the sharp-looking edge.

"See," Leo said to Matilda. "I told you he'd be crazy about it."

Crazy is right, Phillip thought. Just looking at the sword made his throat hurt. All the disappointments of birthdays past came rushing back: the hot-coal-walking kit, the red and yellow striped leotard, the purple unicycle, the snake that almost ate him. He had been polite, said thank you, and pretended to like the circus presents. But this time, his hopes had been too high. He couldn't even force himself to smile. It was so unfair. How could he get his dad to understand that he would never be a circus star?

Phillip jumped up and flung the sword. It sailed straight into one of the wooden posts holding up a tent and stuck fast.

"Wow. Great throw," said Leo. "We can use that in the act."

"I don't want to be in the act," Phillip told him.

"What?" Leo asked.

Phillip didn't want to hurt his dad's feelings, but he couldn't stop himself. His words poured out like clowns from a fallen phone booth.

"I don't want to be in the act, and I don't want to be in the circus. I've tried, but I don't fit in. I want to live in a regular town like a regular kid. Let me stay with Aunt Veola and Uncle Felix."

"I don't know," said Leo, scratching his wig.

"Only for a while," Phillip added. "So I can figure out where I belong."

Einstein stomped, demanding attention. Matilda rubbed his trunk.

"I'll call Veola," she told her husband.

"Let's not rush into this," said Leo. "Pennsylvania is hundreds of miles from here, and we don't even have money for a train ticket."

Phillip asked, "If we did have the money, could I go?"

"Sure," said Leo. "But we don't."

"Yes, we do," said Phillip. He ran over to the post and, using more strength than he thought he had, yanked out the sword. He put it back in the box and handed it to his dad. "If you return my present, we can use the money to buy a ticket."

"I don't know," said Leo.

"Let's let him go," said Matilda. "The boy is right. He needs to understand what the world is like if he's ever to find his place in it. If we make the arrangements quickly, he'll be able to start the new school year in Hardingtown."

Leo shook his head. "Sorry," he said, pushing the box back to Phillip. "I didn't save the receipt."

Phillip sighed and reached for the box, but his mom intercepted it and handed it back to Leo.

"I did," she said.

She pulled the crinkled receipt out of her pocket and held it high. Einstein lifted his trunk and blew. To Phillip, the sound was like a train whistle.

According to circus superstition, when a performer leaves the show, it's bad luck to say good-bye. Unless you want to jinx someone, the only appropriate parting words are, "See you down the road."

"Take care of yourself, son," Leo said to Phillip as they stood on the platform waiting for the Amtrak Limited. Phillip was glad he was not superstitious.

He clutched his ticket to his chest, needing to feel it against his pounding heart to remind himself that this was not a dream. There was a bench next to the train station's tiny ticket booth, but Phillip was so full of nervous energy he thought it better to stand.

Suddenly, a whistle screamed, and the train screeched into the station. A gust of wind from the train's approach almost made Leo's rainbow wig fly off.

Matilda grabbed Phillip and squeezed. For a moment, he thought he might suffocate in the folds of her enormous polka-dot dress.

"Uncle Felix will pick you up," she said. "If he's not there when you arrive, wait for him on the bench under the sign."

Phillip felt mixed up. He wanted to smile and cry at the same time. Of course he was excited to go live with Aunt Veola and Uncle Felix, but would he fit in?

"All aboard," the voice over the loudspeaker said.

Phillip slipped his ticket into his trousers and kissed the teary spot on his mom's cheek. Leo held out his hand for a shake.

"Put it there, son," he said. Phillip pushed back his shoulders, proudly.

Bzzzzz. The hand buzzer made Phillip's whole hand tingle.

"Gotcha!" Leo said. He hit a button on his neck strap and his bow tie spun.

Phillip wondered why his father always dressed and acted like a clown, even when he wasn't performing. He faked a half smile and fumbled with his luggage. Pedro, the elephant trainer, had shown Phillip how to mount an elephant many times. No one had ever taught him how to mount a train. Halfway up the steps to the passenger car, his suitcase fell. On his second try, the circus trunk slid back down. Finally, by holding his suitcase in front of him and bouncing it up one step at a time, while dragging his circus trunk behind him, Phillip mounted the train.

"See you down the road," his mom called.

"And remember," his dad added, "it's better to have your eye on the ball than a ball in your eye."

Phillip waved good-bye from the window by his seat. He was one of a handful of people on the train. The man seated closest to him snored. The ride itself felt like any one of the Windy Van Hooten Circus trucks, but it gave him excited goose bumps. He wasn't stealing through the darkness to another nameless place to put on the same boring show. He was heading toward a new life, in broad daylight, with his eyes open, and anything was possible.

The world flew past his window. Scattered houses turned into trees, which grew into thick forests. The forests thinned into meadows, which bloomed with wildflowers, which brought grazing cows. The cows dwindled, replaced by barking dogs in fenced yards behind scattered houses. The houses crowded closer together as yards shrank into spaces barely big enough to hold them.

"Hardingtown Station," the conductor called. "Next stop Hardingtown Station."

Phillip jumped from his seat. He dragged his luggage down the aisle and pushed open the exit door.

The platform where the two cars were joined together trembled like an inexperienced lion tamer. He tested it as if it were a tightrope, then held onto a metal wall handle for support. Through the glass on the door, he saw his faint reflection staring back. He was too skinny. His thick red hair stuck up in the back. His metal-framed eyeglasses jutted from huge ears. They sat clumsily on his short, pointy nose, which had a single freckle at the end. Phillip stuck out his tongue. His glasses slid down his nose.

"Hardingtown Station," the conductor called. "All off for Hardingtown Station."

Phillip was proud of himself for being first in line. He was off to a great start. No more square peg in a round hole. No more running from clowns throwing pies. No more tripping over his own two feet. Now, to get off the train without falling down the steps.

WELCOME TO HARDINGTOWN

THE UNOFFICIAL

DODGEBALL CAPITAL OF THE WORLD

HOST OF THE ANNUAL DODGEBALL

WORLD SERIES AND BARBECUE

HOME TO THE AMERICAN DODGEBALL COMPANY

VISIT THE HISTORICAL DODGEBALL MUSEUM

Phillip saw the big sign as the door opened. Dodgeball? He wondered what that was.

He sat on a bench and watched people rush around. The weather was dreary for late August. A fog had moved in and covered Phillip's new town with mist. When he realized he was the only person left, he reached for the snack bag his parents had packed.

Phoomp!

A long, green, slinky snake shot from the bag. He could hear his dad's chuckles, even though there were now two hundred miles between them.

Phillip checked out his bag: a cold hot dog, peanuts, and a candy apple. All his favorites, yet they seemed different without the blaring circus music and smell of greasepaint. Like they were old and stale. He nibbled the hot dog, trying to make it last.

He wondered what he should do if Uncle Felix never came.

Once a circus dog learns to ride a bicycle, it's hard to stop him. But it takes the trainer a long time to teach the dog to ride. The trick, his mom once told Phillip, is to realize it's no trick. It's a matter of patience.

Phillip was losing patience, waiting for Uncle Felix to pick him up at the Hardingtown Station. He tried to remember what Uncle Felix looked like from the time he and Aunt Veola had visited the circus when Phillip was five years old. No use. All the men passing by, in their noncircus clothes, looked alike.

Phillip saw a woman approach. She wore a tan raincoat and a serious expression. Her dark brown hair was pulled back tight. Accompanied by her stocky body, the hairstyle made her look like a juggling pin. Phillip thought he should ask her the time.

"You must be Phillip," she said. She removed a plain white handkerchief from her pocket and wiped her hand with it. "I'm Aunt Veola."

She shook Phillip's hand with a firm grip, then wiped her hand again.

"You can catch a cold from a handshake," she explained as she slipped the handkerchief back into her pocket. Phillip liked the look of her face. Add a few more chins and it had the same shape as his mom's.

"Your Uncle Felix was supposed to pick you up over a half hour ago. Don't ask me how a man who has lived in Hardingtown all his life could get lost on his way to the train station, but he managed."

Phillip felt he should say something clever to make a good impression.

"I'm assuming this is yours," she said, tapping her shoe against his suitcase. He nodded.

"That one, too?" she asked, pointing at the trunk. Phillip nodded again, hating his shyness.

"I hope we have enough drawers," she said. As they walked toward the station steps, she asked, "You do know how to talk?"

He nodded. "I mean, yes."

"Your Uncle Felix has the opposite problem," she said. "He never knows when to stop talking." They reached the parking lot and loaded the trunk of her brown sedan.

"I'll take the long route so you can get a look at downtown Hardingtown," she said. Phillip had never seen a city close up before. The Windy Van Hooten Circus caravan bypassed cities to avoid traffic, and the circus tents were set up on the outskirts.

How crowded Hardingtown was, with its rows of sturdy, multistoried buildings. Trees dotted the wide sidewalks, their trunks shooting up from tiny squares of dirt surrounded by yards of concrete. Traffic lights shouted orders at obedient cars while streams of people rushed through crosswalks.

Phillip rolled down his window. The grind of car engines and tidbits of conversations floated through the sedan. The fresh brew of a coffee shop mixed with the fumes from a dump truck. Near a busy intersection was a large, domed building. To Phillip, it looked like there were a zillion steps leading up to it. People were rushing in and out. Many were dressed in business suits and carrying briefcases.

"That's the courthouse," Aunt Veola said, "where I work. You'll meet me there after school each day. When I get off at five-thirty, we'll drive home together."

"Where's the school?" he asked.

"Four blocks that way." She pointed down a side street. "You'll see it in the morning."

Phillip pushed his glasses up his nose and smiled. Tomorrow was August 30, the first day of school. His mom had enrolled him as a sixth-grade student at Hardingtown Middle School, the same school she and Aunt Veola had attended.

"Over there is Newman's Trophies," Aunt Veola said, pointing to a storefront.

Phillip gazed at the trophy shop. In the window was a giant silver statue of a man in a victorious pose.

"What's that?" he asked.

"That," said Aunt Veola, "is the most coveted prize in Hardingtown—the Dodgeball Master Championship Trophy." It was three feet high and took up most of the window. "They award it once a year," she explained, "on the last day of the Annual Dodgeball World Series and Barbecue." Even from the rear window, as the shop began to shrink with the distance, the trophy looked huge.

"Over there is the Hardingtown Hotel," she said. "That's where your Uncle Felix used to work. He was a valet. Do you know what a valet is?"

Phillip shook his head.

"He parked cars for the hotel guests. When the hotel lot was full, his job was to find another place in the city to park the cars. Nearly a year, he worked there. Then he forgot where he parked a couple of the cars, and they fired him." She clicked on the sedan's left-turn signal. "He's got a job as a seam inspector at the factory now. You can see the smokestack from here."

Phillip looked off to his right. The smokestack jutted out from above the roofs of the well-maintained row homes. It had neon letters that lit up one at a time. A-M-E-R-I-C-A-N D-O-D-G-E-B-A-L-L C-O-M-P-A-N-Y.

Phillip remembered the train station sign: THE UNOFFICIAL DODGEBALL CAPITAL OF THE WORLD.

"What is dodgeball?" he asked.

The car jerked to a stop.

"Dodgeball is Hardingtown, and Hardingtown is dodgeball," Aunt Veola declared. Phillip gave her the same blank expression he used to give his dad when he told a new joke. A car began blowing its horn, and she accelerated.

"I thought it was some kind of a game," Phillip said.

"Of course it's a game," said Aunt Veola. "But here in Hardingtown it's more than that. The American Dodgeball Company is the city's biggest employer. There is no greater honor in Hardingtown than being inducted into the Historical Dodgeball Museum's Hall of Fame. If you want to get along around here, you'll have to play."

That was the end of it. They continued in silence.

Aunt Veola pulled the sedan off the main street and through an alley. A sharp turn led up a steep hill. Houses lined the side of the hill like a staircase. Cars were crammed together in front. Aunt Veola found an empty space near a narrow, Victorian-style row home.

"This is it," she announced. The brightness of Aunt Veola's clean white house made the dirty white houses on both sides look gray.

Inside, it smelled like disinfectant. Aunt Veola gave Phillip a tour. The whole time she was pointing out the kitchen and the laundry room and the pantry, Phillip heard an echo—"If you want to get along around here, you'll have to play."

When she showed him his bedroom, Phillip noticed a picture of his mom on his nightstand.

"So you won't get too homesick," explained Aunt Veola. Phillip had never seen his mom looking so young. She was wearing a red knit sweater embroidered with the initials H.H.

As he fell asleep that night Phillip couldn't help but wonder: Why had his mom never told him about dodgeball?

Circus lingo is confusing to outsiders. For example, a circus cookhouse is called a pie car. But the term "cherry pie" means doing extra work for extra pay. If you go to the pie car and order cherry, you're likely to be washing dishes on an empty stomach.

Phillip found noncircus lingo equally confusing. "Cat got your tongue?" Uncle Felix asked him between bites of crunchy breakfast cereal the next morning. A fruity puff dripped off the edge of his mouth and landed back in his bowl. He was a thick-necked man with ferociously curly blond hair that made his head look huge. Together with his chunky torso, skinny legs, and petite feet, it created a strangely shaped body that resembled an upside-down juggling pin. Exactly the opposite of Aunt Veola and, yet, a perfect upside-down fit.

Uncle Felix's lips rested so little, Phillip wondered if he talked in his sleep.

"Huh?" Phillip asked.

"I know you're probably nervous about starting school this morning. But let your wise old uncle set your mind at ease." He cocked his finger and pointed it at Phillip like a water pistol. "You're going to have a great first day."

Phillip sighed. "I hope so."

"I know so," said Uncle Felix. "I remember my first day of fifth grade like it was yesterday. One of the best days of my life."

"You mean sixth grade," said Phillip.

"No. I mean fifth grade. My first day of sixth grade was a complete disaster."

"But I'm going into sixth grade," said Phillip.

"Oh, sorry," said Uncle Felix. "I forgot." He passed Phillip the box of cereal. "Better eat. Don't want your stomach grumbling all morning."

Phillip sprinkled cereal into his bowl while Uncle Felix recited the list of vitamins and minerals the box promised in every serving. The tiny, hard balls pounded against the ceramic with clinking sounds. He poured in milk and watched the balls floating. Phillip always lost his appetite when he was worried about something. But he didn't want to make stomach noises.

"Go on," said Uncle Felix, "fill 'er up."

Phillip forced the spoon into his mouth and chewed. The cereal was too sweet, and the milk tasted like it was about to go bad.

"Haven't thought of my first day of sixth grade in a long time," said Uncle Felix. "Everything that could go wrong did. First, I wore the wrong clothes. Completely out of style."

Phillip looked at his blue jeans and plain gray T-shirt. Was he dressed okay? His ears felt warmer, like they always did when he got nervous or upset.

"Then, I lost my lunch money and had to borrow from the office."

Phillip thought about a hole he had in the pocket of his jeans. Which side had he put his money into? He took a paper napkin from a holder on the table and wiped his sweaty forehead.

"Then, when I got to science class, there was this horrible smell, and I threw up all over the science teacher."

Phillip dropped his spoon. It whopped into his bowl, sending milk splattering. His ears were so hot they felt sunburned.

"I have to go," Phillip said, darting from his chair. "I don't want to be late."

"Good idea," said Uncle Felix. "You'll get detention if you're late."

Phillip rushed to the front door.

"If you ever need to talk about your worries again . . ." Uncle Felix called after him. Phillip was out the door before he could hear anything more.

As soon as he got down the hill, he felt better. The walk to school gave him a chance to cool down. Aunt Veola had written him directions to Hardingtown Middle School and he found it with ease. But once he was close up, the three-story brick building seemed huge and intimidating.

The inside was even worse. It was a maze of halls and classrooms. The "map" the office woman gave him did not show the floor plan. It only listed subjects and numbers. Phillip wondered what the numbers meant.

A bell rang and children hurried into classrooms. Then it was quiet. Phillip crept down the hall peering into each window. The rooms were large. So were the students. Everything seemed huge, except him.

"Hey, you," a deep voice boomed.

Phillip swung around so quickly he practically knocked the voice over. It belonged to a lanky girl with shoulder-length black hair. She was wearing khaki pants and a red T-shirt with a big checkmark at the top. A faded blue sash hung from her left shoulder to her right hip.

"Get to class," she said.

Phillip froze. The girl took a step closer.

"I said, get to class."

Phillip looked at the classroom to his left and the one to his right. Either one had to be better than staying in the hall.

"Give me your schedule," the girl snapped.

"My what?" Phillip asked.

"Your schedule," she repeated. "Your class schedule."

"You mean my map?" he asked, holding the paper up. The girl snatched it.

"First Period, English," she read. "Room 209. It's over there."

"Thank you, Hall," Phillip said.

"What did you call me?" she asked. Phillip looked at the name patch sewn on her blue sash. The end of it was curled inward so that he could not read the entire thing.

"Hall," he said.

"Are you trying to be a wise guy?"

"No. Your name tag says Hall. Isn't that your name?" The girl glanced down at her sash and swept the drooping patch back.

Hall Monitor.

"My name," she said, "is B.B. Tyson. And, for your information, nobody makes fun of B.B. Tyson." She held the schedule out and let it drop to the floor. "Get to class." B.B. turned and stomped off.

Phillip scooped up the paper and raced to room 209. Once he got settled in his seat, his breathing returned to normal. He noticed the kids raised their hands before speaking. They also handed one another papers rolled into triangles. Mr. Morton, a thin-haired man with a long beard, was talking and holding up books they would be required to read.

He took a piece of squeaky chalk and wrote on the board: _The Adventures of Huckleberry Finn, by Mark Twain._ Groans were heard, although Phillip, who had already read the novel, was pleased. When his mom tutored him, he read one piece of classical literature each week. Reading was his favorite subject.

By the end of class, the churning in Phillip's stomach was gone. The kid behind him told Phillip how to find his next classroom. The class after that, he found on his own.

At lunch, someone asked what school he went to before. Phillip didn't want the kids to know about his circus past, so he only said he had a tutor. A group of kids in polo shirts let him sit with them. They talked about preparatory academies. They asked him what it was like to have a private tutor. He said it was lonely, especially since he had no brothers or sisters. After that, Phillip mostly ate his watery spaghetti, nodded, and smiled.

In geography, Phillip raised his hand when a teacher asked where was Walla Walla. He knew the answer was the state of Washington because the Windy Van Hooten Circus had been there. But the teacher had called on the girl sitting in front of him.

Phillip checked his schedule. His last class was gym. What was gym? There was no classroom number listed. Phillip turned down a new hallway. He saw double doors. The glass in the doors was covered in wire netting. Above the doors it said GYMNASIUM. Phillip looked inside. It was like a circus arena without the tent. In the center was a performing area. Basketball hoops hung from the sides. A knotted rope spilled down from the ceiling in the corner. Boys and girls sat on the bleachers that lined the walls. Phillip went in and sat with them.

A man wearing a black baseball cap was in front of the crowd. He had a dimpled chin and a silver whistle that hung from a string around his neck. When he blew the whistle to quiet the crowd, Phillip half expected to see clowns ride unicycles onto the floor. The man introduced himself as the coach and told them they would have gym class every Monday. He talked about gym clothes and teamwork and pushing hard. He had a clipboard. Each time he said something, he would raise his clipboard and make a mark. After he was done, he asked if there were questions. Phillip thought about asking why the gym smelled like dirty socks when everyone had their shoes on but decided against it.

Coach looked at his watch.

"We still have fifteen minutes. Let's play a little dodgeball," he said. "Count off."

Phillip heard the kids around him. "One." "Two." "One." "Two," they said. When the kid next to him said, "One," Phillip said, "Two."

"Ones on the left. Twos on the right," said Coach. The group split in half, and the kids went to opposite sides of the gym. Coach placed three balls along a line in the middle of the gym. The stiff, inflatable balls were made of the kind of hard, grooved rubber that looked like it could remove skin at high speeds.

Coach blew his whistle.

Kids from both sides ran to grab the balls. One kid tumbled head over heels as another beat him to a ball. The kid who got the ball cocked his tongue and threw the ball over the line at the other team. To Phillip, the players looked like clowns chasing one another around the circus ring, throwing custard pies.

A kid jumped with both feet as a ball whizzed past ankle-high. His teammate grabbed the ball and sent it zooming back. A petite girl with a ponytail took it in the side and splattered onto the floor.

"You're out," Coach yelled. The girl crawled to the bleachers. The boy who threw the ball chuckled.

It reminded Phillip of the time his dad had given him the unicycle. As soon as he managed to balance himself, the clowns began chasing him, throwing pies. He hid from them on the trapeze platform for hours, until Bartholomew the Giant finally came and helped him down. Phillip still had nightmares about clowns throwing pies, trying to land one on his kisser. Nothing frightened him more than the thought of lemon meringue stuck in his nostrils. Until now.

Each time a kid got hit, Coach yelled, "Out!" and pointed. The kid who got hit would have to sit on the bleachers. Phillip could practically see the whipped cream streaming down their humiliated faces. He could hardly believe that kids with balls were purposely aiming at ones without them.

Whap! A boy standing near the line got it in the gut.

Whack! A girl who had turned to run got it in the back.

A ball zipped so close to Phillip, he could hear the air scream. The girl next to him twisted to avoid a low ball. She slipped, and the ball hit her as she lay on the ground. A circular red spot formed on her exposed back thigh before she staggered away.

Phillip had lost three-quarters of his team. Fewer kids meant more balls thrown his way. He caught a glimpse of the clock. Maybe he could survive until the bell. He backed himself into the far corner.

"Get the new kid," a familiar voice yelled. It was B.B. Tyson, the hall monitor. She lobbed a screamer right at him. It barely missed. There was no place to go. Phillip's head brushed against the rope hanging from the ceiling. He jumped for the rope, grabbed the end, and began yanking himself up as fast as he could. B.B. unleashed another screamer at him.

"Get him!" she hollered. A ball zoomed by as he climbed. The rope swung, making him harder to hit. Closer to the ceiling, the balls dropped short of him. He was safe.

"Hey, Tarzan," yelled B.B. She tossed her ball and beat her chest.

"*AhhhAhhAhhhaaaa!*" she roared.

"It's George of the Jungle," another kid shouted.

Phillip surveyed the herd of sixth-graders. Most of the kids who weren't making fun of him were bent over with laughter.

Coach blew his whistle.

"That's enough," he said. As if on cue, the bell rang, and the pack of howling children raced out of the gym.

They were all gone.

Phillip breathed a sigh of relief. Until he realized he was still twenty feet in the air and, like a cat stuck in a tree, afraid to climb down.

6

Bartholomew the Giant was three feet, eight inches tall. If he had called himself Bartholomew the Midget, people would have expected less of him. A short midget was nothing special, he used to explain, but a miniature giant was unique.

Phillip felt anything but special in the line at the Harding-town County Courthouse. He was in the security area of the lobby. Aunt Veola had said to meet at the courthouse after school, but he had forgotten to ask her where. Would he be able to find her?

In front of him was a row of dark suits shuffling toward a metal detector. The guard stopped a man with a buzzing belt buckle.

"You can hide a pocketknife behind a belt buckle," Phillip heard the guard explain in a serious voice as the man was made to remove it. The beltless man went through the detector. Did Phillip have anything metal on? He wasn't sure.

A female construction worker in steel-toed boots was next to make the thing sing. The guard tapped on her shoes and heard the ping of the steel-toed tips. "You can hide a bullet in a boot," the guard said solemnly as the woman was made to strip to her socks.

Phillip stayed close to the man in front of him. The man removed his pocket change and keys. He placed them in a plastic box on a table. They entered the detector together. It went off. The man hopped out, leaving Phillip standing there.

"Hello, Phillip," the guard said. "How was your day at school?"

"Aunt Veola?" asked Phillip, surprised to see her in a courthouse guard uniform. She wore a crisp white shirt with a shoulder patch that said HARDINGTOWN COUNTY SHERIFF'S DEPARTMENT. Her black leather security belt held a walkie-talkie, a key chain, a leather pouch, a nightstick, and a half dozen other scary-looking things.

"You, over here," Aunt Veola said gravely to the man in front of Phillip. She swept a handheld device over him.

"You can hide a razor blade behind your calf," she explained in earnest.

"Yes, ma'am," the man said, stepping aside.

"And you," she said to Phillip. "You need to go around the metal detector. Not through it."

"Okay," Phillip said, backing out and going around.

"Those darn things are loaded with radiation poisoning," she confided. "Every time you pass through, you lose brain cells. Understand?"

"I guess," Phillip said. He knew from his science studies that it probably wasn't true, but he wanted to be polite.

"Do you want your fingers to turn black?"

"No," he answered.

"Do you want your toes to fall off?"

"No," he answered again.

"Go on, then," she said. "Up to the snack bar, and wait for me there."

She held out a crisp dollar bill. Phillip took the money and looked down the hallway for the snack-bar sign.

"Next one through," he heard Aunt Veola say. A man in a blue suit stood still as a statue, staring at the ominous frame of the metal detector. "Let's go," she said impatiently. "What are you afraid of?"

Phillip headed to the snack bar for his after-school snack. It was a dingy little place with a dozen tables balanced on uneven legs and a long counter, which a young woman was wiping with a rag. Hanging behind her was a menu with prices.

For one dollar, Phillip could get a small bowl of soup, a grilled-cheese sandwich, or something called "the Dodgeballburger." The woman at the counter explained to Phillip that the Dodgeballburger was a meatball with tomato sauce on a hamburger roll. Phillip chose a can of root beer from the cooler and a bag of chips.

The man behind the cash register was broad-shouldered. His skin was as close to pitch-black as Phillip had ever seen. He had thick muscles bulging out of his shirt and slightly graying hair. He wore cool sunglasses—the kind that have mirrors for lenses, so when you look at him you're looking back at yourself. There was a tag pinned to his shirt that said MY NAME IS SAM, but after his *Hall Monitor* mistake, Phillip wasn't about to jump to any conclusions.

"Hello," the man said. "What do you have there?"

"A bag of chips," said Phillip. The man hit a key on the cash register.

"Fifty cents," the cash register said. Phillip smiled. He had never heard a talking cash register.

"What else do you have?"

"A can of root beer," said Phillip. The man hit another key.

"Fifty cents," the cash register said.

"Is that it?" the man asked.

"That's all," said Phillip.

"Your total is one dollar," the cash register said. The man held out his hand, and Phillip placed the dollar bill in it. The man hit another key, and the drawer to the cash register opened.

"You have zero change," the cash register said.

"That is so cool," said Phillip.

"Have a nice day," the man replied. Phillip looked around at the tables.

"Is there any ketchup?"

"What for?"

"My potato chips."

"I'll bring a bottle out."

Phillip made himself comfortable at a table near a window. The chair made a squeak each time he leaned forward to sip his root beer.

"You know," said the cashier, who was suddenly standing next to him holding a ketchup bottle, "you're only the second person I've ever met who dips potato chips in ketchup. You wouldn't happen to be related to Veola, would you?"

"She's my aunt," said Phillip.

"So you're Veola's nephew. She told me you were coming to live with her. My name is Sam." He held out his hand. Phillip shook it, like Aunt Veola had shaken his.

"I'm Phillip."

"You seem kind of down in the dumps, Phillip."

"How did you know that?"

"Your tone of voice."

"I had a rough day," Phillip admitted.

"Sounds like the new-kid blues. It's hard to get used to a strange new place," said Sam. "Especially Hardingtown."

"Does everybody in Hardingtown play dodgeball?" Phillip asked.

"They don't call it the tuna-fish capital of the world," said Sam. He went back to his cash register and rang up a smiling woman's order. He chatted with the customers as he worked, and they returned his friendliness. He seemed like the kind of guy you could talk to. When Sam was done, he came back to Phillip's table, the smell of Dodgeballburgers still clinging to his shirt.

"Can I ask you a question, Sam?"

"Go ahead."

"When you were a kid, did you ever feel like you were . . ." Phillip searched for the right words. ". . . like you were different?"

"Sure. We're all different," said Sam. "That's what makes us so much alike."

"That doesn't make any sense," said Phillip.

"Yes, it does. Look at you and me. We're about a world apart. We don't look alike. We don't sound alike. We don't act alike. But already we're friends."

"I guess," said Phillip.

"I'll make you a deal," Sam said. "Anytime you need someone to share your problems with, you come see me. Anytime I need someone to share my problems with, I'll come see you."

Phillip could hardly imagine how this strong, dark man with the confident smile could ever need him for anything.

Still, the thought that he had made a friend did make him feel better. So what if Sam wasn't a kid his own age? Sam was cool.

"Should we have a secret handshake?" Phillip asked.

"How about a secret signal. A sound of some sort?" suggested Sam.

Phillip liked the idea. He was used to signals. The Windy Van Hooten Circus band would play John Philip Sousa's "The Stars and Stripes Forever" whenever they wanted to warn the circus workers that something was wrong. Phillip picked up the salt and pepper shakers and banged them together.

Clink.

"That's good," said Sam. "Anytime you need to talk, you give the signal and I'll come over."

Phillip had a friend. He could hardly wait to tell Aunt Veola. During the car ride home, she wanted to hear about his day. He told her he had played his first dodgeball game. He skipped the part about climbing the rope and getting stuck and the janitor bringing a ladder. Then he told her he had made a friend who looked like he would be good at sports. Maybe he could give Phillip tips on dodgeball.

"What's the boy's name?" she asked.

"He's not a boy," Phillip explained. "I met him at the courthouse. His name is Sam."

"Sam what?"

"I don't know his last name," said Phillip.

"The only Sam I know who works in the courthouse is Sam Phoenix. He's the cashier at the snack bar," she said. "But Sam couldn't give anyone tips on how to dodge balls."

"Why not?" Phillip asked.

Aunt Veola replied, "Sam Phoenix is blind."

Lions are not smart and are easily distracted. When a lion is about to attack, the trainer will crack his whip. When it hears the noise, the lion will forget what it was thinking and will not attack.

The next day, Phillip smiled at anyone who looked his way. He hoped that if he distracted his classmates with his friendly personality, they would forget that he was a complete idiot in gym class. It was not working.

"B.B. is going to murder you for that Tarzan stunt," a kid warned. "She doesn't like to lose."

"I didn't make her lose," Phillip said.

"You made it a tie. If there's anybody not out on the other team when the bell rings, it's a tie. B.B. hates ties."

The week was a blur. Phillip got up, dressed, and went to classes. After school, he went to the cafeteria and ordered a root beer and chips and did his homework. All he could think about was how to survive his next dodgeball game.

Suddenly, it was Monday.

"If I were you," a smaller kid told him, "I'd lie down and let her hit me."

"That way you get it over with," agreed another kid.

Phillip thought about it. "I couldn't do that," he decided.

"Then you're gonna get creamed," the smaller kid said. Phillip imagined a banana-cream dodgeball speeding toward him.

"Look on the bright side," said the other kid. "It couldn't be any worse."

The bell rang and Phillip went to lunch. Today's menu was meat loaf. Phillip tried to eat as much as he could, but he wasn't hungry. He was so lost in his thoughts, he didn't notice when he approached the table where B.B. and her friends were sitting. Suddenly, Phillip tripped. His tray full of leftover food flew up.

Crrrashhhh!!!

Wrinkled peas and bits of syrupy meat loaf rained down on B.B. Tyson and her friends. Globs of sticky brown meat clung to B.B's hair. A piece of smelly garlic bread perched on her left ear.

"Stanislaw!" B.B. screamed. A gooey pea skied down her nose and fell off the tip. "You'd better start shopping for a tombstone."

Fifth period came and went too soon. Everyone knew B.B. would be trying to whack him in gym. The whole school was placing bets on how long he would last. Phillip marched to gym class as if in a funeral procession. Should he climb the rope again? In the gym, Phillip saw the rope had been tied up and off to the side, out of reach.

The kids counted off. It occurred to Phillip that if he and B.B. were on the same team she wouldn't be allowed to hit him with the ball. It must have occurred to her, too. She made sure she sat next to him.

"One," said B.B.

"Two," said Phillip.

The game began. Balls flew and rivals squared off. Phillip scurried to the wall farthest from the line separating the teams. He watched the smaller kids. Some ran. Some dodged. Most tried to hide behind bigger kids. Phillip scanned the gym for a good place to hide. That's when he saw Shawn O'Malley. He was the fattest kid in school. Big as an oak, with legs like tree trunks planted firmly into the floor. Why had nobody else thought to hide behind Shawn? Phillip all but disappeared behind him. B.B. will never find me now, Phillip thought.

A ball zipped across the room and beamed a kid in the gut. He skid across the floor on his backside. Shawn held his belly and laughed. Over Shawn's lowered shoulder, Phillip spotted B.B. rearing back with the ball. Shawn didn't even see it coming. The hard orb blasted his left shoulder and knocked Shawn off balance.

It happened as if in slow motion. For a fraction of a second, Shawn teetered. His weight tilted forward. It shifted to the tips of his toes, then back to the balls of his feet. Finally, he toppled backward. Straight back.

Down.

Down.

All two hundred and five pounds of him.

Lucky for Shawn, Phillip was between him and the cold, hard floor. Not so lucky for Phillip, who stuck his hand out to break his fall. He heard himself scream as his wrist twisted backward.

An hour later, Phillip was in the school nurse's office waiting for Uncle Felix. The ice on his wrist made him shiver. It was almost worse than the throbbing pain. He wanted to complain, but Coach was standing there and would call him a wuss. Coach had already lectured him on why not to hide behind a fat kid with poor equilibrium during dodgeball.

"Got here as fast as I could," said Uncle Felix as he entered the room. He removed his cowboy hat, and messy blond curls spilled onto his forehead. He knelt next to Phillip and inspected his wrist.

"Are you okay?" he asked.

"I think it's broken," Phillip said, trying not to tear up.

"More likely it's a mild sprain," the school nurse explained. "But you might want to get it X-rayed if the swelling keeps up."

"How'd it happen?"

"Gym class," Coach said. "The boy trips over his own two feet."

"Some kids aren't athletic," the nurse agreed.

"This one's something special," Coach said. "You'd think he'd never played organized sports before."

"Well," Uncle Felix said, "coming from a circus family, there's not a lot of that."

Phillip felt a flush rush through his body, so hot it nearly melted the ice on his wrist.

"Circus family?" asked Coach.

Please stop talking, thought Phillip. Please stop. All his life he'd waited for a chance to be part of a normal family in a regular town. If the kids at school found out about his weird circus family, how would he ever be one of them, ever fit in?

"Sure," continued Uncle Felix. He sat in a chair next to the nurse's desk. "Phillip comes from a diverse line of circus performers. The Stupendous Stanislaws, they're called."

"Why, isn't that cute. Did you ever do any circus stunts?" the nurse asked Phillip.

"Not Phillip," Uncle Felix said. "He was too young for a serious act. Mostly he shoveled the elephant pens and worked the pooper-scooper during shows."

Phillip wanted to melt into liquid and leak under his chair. He wanted to stay there until he had evaporated completely and was gone.

"Don't you have to get back to work?" Phillip asked.

"I forgot." Uncle Felix laughed. "We should get going."

Twice on the drive home, Phillip opened his mouth to ask Uncle Felix not to tell anyone else about his circus past. But his uncle was talking about his younger days as the mascot for the Hardingtown Hedgehogs and never paused long enough to let him get in a word.

"I had this great stuffed dodgeball costume," Uncle Felix said, "with this hedgehog hanging off the front. I'd run around in front of the stands during the halftime show, pretending I was getting thrown. The crowd loved me." He talked about flirting with Aunt Veola at dodgeball matches where she was the Official Team Scorekeeper. "Even back then, she was a no-nonsense gal," he said, "but I could make her smile."

Uncle Felix talked. And talked. And talked. Phillip was polite and listened, but, in fact, he could hardly breathe.

"Breathe in. Breathe out," Mario the stilt-walker would tell Phillip when he became nervous.

Phillip remembered how the children in the stands during the circus shows used to look at his family, gawking at his mom and laughing at his dad. You have to be like everyone else to fit in, Phillip thought. I can't let them know I'm a circus freak.

"Please," Phillip blurted out. "Don't tell people I was raised in the circus."

"Why would I do that?" Uncle Felix asked.

"You just did. You told Coach."

"Sorry," Uncle Felix said. "I didn't know it was a secret."

Phillip was glad he'd spoken up. He felt his lungs relaxing.

"Nothing wrong with having a little secret," Uncle Felix continued, giving Phillip a wink. "Got plenty of my own. As I always say, what Veola doesn't know won't hurt me."

Phillip took the ice pack off his wrist and set it aside.

"Set your mind at ease, little nephew. I'm an expert at keeping secrets. Nothing like Coach. Why, when we were growing up together, we used to call him Blabbermouth Tyson. He could spread a rumor faster than a hedgehog on a highway."

Phillip grabbed the ice pack and put it on his head, where a giant headache was beginning to form. Maybe it would be better not to share his worries with Uncle Felix. But he had a bigger problem to deal with now. How could he stop Coach from blabbing?

8

Tigers don't wear circus costumes. Horses, camels, monkeys, even elephants can all be outfitted, no matter how ridiculously, to suit the performer's fancy. But you cannot force a big cat into a tutu.

Coach reminded Phillip of a tiger. He was strong, brave, and probably didn't like other people trying to tell him what to do. Still, Phillip knew he would have to convince Coach to keep his circus life a secret.

Phillip's alarm clock went off at 5:30 A.M. He would get to school early when the teachers started showing up for work. Then he could find Coach and explain. Surely Coach would understand. There would be no end to the teasing he would have to endure if his schoolmates found out that he was an elephant-poop shoveler. He would be different. They would never accept him.

Phillip located the teachers' parking lot. He stood next to a dogwood tree near the sidewalk leading to the back door. The first teacher to arrive was Peter Periwinkle, the home economics teacher. He was a painfully skinny man who glided rather than walked. He typically carried fully loaded tote bags in his hands. Kids said the bags were full of rocks to prevent Mr. Periwinkle from being blown away by a strong wind.

Next, he saw Elizabeth Castapio, an auburn-haired student teacher, who helped in the chemistry lab. Miss Castapio's classes were full of boys who became motivated to immerse themselves in science after catching the scent of her honeysuckle perfume in the hallway.

Finally, a red Mustang pulled up, and Phillip saw Coach get out. As Phillip moved in Coach's direction, the passenger door flew open and B.B. Tyson exited. Coach went around to the back and opened the trunk. B.B. pulled out her backpack and slipped it on.

"Breathe in and out. In and out," Phillip reminded himself, feeling faint.

Coach, he realized, was B.B's father. They headed for the sidewalk. Phillip wished he could freeze them in place to decide what to do. What if Coach had already told B.B.? That was too horrible to think about. Phillip hid behind the tree until they entered the building. Then he went around to the front.

Twenty-five minutes later, the halls were bustling with the sounds of kids chatting and lockers slamming. One group repeated jokes from a television show. Another group gossiped about the couple caught kissing under the bleachers during a recreational dodgeball game the night before.

Phillip began to loosen up. Maybe he had been making a big deal out of nothing. Coach probably wouldn't even remember his conversation with Uncle Felix. Besides, thought Phillip, I couldn't be the first kid in school to have been in the circus.

Brrrrrriiing!

The warning bell was right on schedule. Phillip hurried to his locker. He tried to turn the combination with his hurt wrist.

"Ouch."

"Let me get that for you," said a tall student. He looked familiar. Phillip watched as the tall kid twirled the spinner until the door popped open.

"Thanks," he said.

"No, thank you," the tall kid said.

"For what?"

"For breaking my cousin's fall."

Phillip pictured Shawn falling backward onto him. The family resemblance was slight.

"Seriously," the tall kid said. "Shawn's got poor equilibrium. Bad balance. He told me you tried to catch him. That's cool." The tall kid slapped Phillip on the back and walked away.

Cool? Phillip repeated. Did that tall kid call me cool?

Phillip was going to keep a positive attitude. He would smile all day. He would say hello. So what if they didn't respond? He grabbed his books and headed for homeroom. B.B. and her girlfriends were coming in the opposite direction. He suppressed the urge to run. He was cool. He would say hello.

"Hello," Phillip said.

"Hey, circus boy," said B.B. "Shovel any elephant poop lately?" Her friends howled with laughter. Phillip dropped his books and raced down the hallway. He darted into the boys' bathroom.

Brrrrrriiing!

The late bell. Phillip knew he should be in class. But he couldn't face the other kids. B.B. knew. They all knew. As soon as the hallway was quiet, Phillip sneaked down the steps and ran out of the school.

Once the Windy Van Hooten Circus was low on cash and had to let some employees go. When the tightrope walker was told he had lost his job, he asked the owner how he was supposed to get home to his family. The owner pointed to a string of telephone poles. "You can walk," he said.

The whole way from school to the courthouse, Phillip thought about going back home to his family. He had to get away from Hardingtown.

"What are you doing here?" asked Aunt Veola, checking the courthouse clock. "Are you sick?"

She removed a thin, latex glove from the pouch on her security belt, snapped it on, and felt his forehead. Phillip pulled away. He used his shirtsleeve to wipe his eyes. It left a dirty streak across his face.

"I don't want to live in Hardingtown," Phillip said.

"You're having a bad day, that's all. It's hard to adjust to a new school," she said.

"I'll never fit in here."

"Give it more time, Phillip."

"No. I want to see my parents. Call my mom and tell her I want to come home."

"I can't do that, Phillip," Aunt Veola said.

Phillip felt as if an elephant had fallen on him. "Why not?" he asked.

"Because I promised your mother I would take care of you. You've only been here a week. You haven't even given it a chance."

"I want to go home."

"This is your home for now," said Aunt Veola. "You're going to have to make the best of it." Tears trickled down Phillip's face. Aunt Veola removed a pack of facial tissues from a zippered compartment in her security jacket.

"You can wear a rut in your face from crying too much," she said. She handed him a tissue to blot his tears away. "You should wash up before you go back to school."

In the restroom, the cold water stung Phillip's exhausted eyes. Aunt Veola didn't understand. It wasn't just the circus teasing. There was the dodgeball problem, too.

Phillip considered his options.

#1—Go back to school and give B.B. another chance to hit him so hard his entire body would explode with such force that Mr. Vanderburg, the custodian, would take a week to mop him off the gymnasium walls.

#2—Go back to Aunt Veola's house, jump into bed, hide under the covers, and refuse to go to school, after which a truant officer would lock him in jail, where he would be forced to eat cockroaches to survive.

#3—Run away.

It was time to pack his bags. Phillip heard his stomach rumble. Before he left, he would go to the snack bar for something to eat.

The snack bar was crowded and smelled like the Sauerkraut Bagel special. Phillip sat at a table to wait the line out. The salt-and-pepper shakers on the table seemed to stare at him. He picked them up and thought about the secret signal. Even if he told Sam what had happened, there was nothing a blind man could do. There was nothing anyone could do. Phillip was all alone. He put the shakers down, grabbed a bag of potato chips and a root beer, and got in line.

"Good morning," said Sam.

"Morning," Phillip answered. He made his voice sound lower, like a man's voice.

"No school today, Phillip?" Sam asked.

"I'm on a field trip," he answered, surprised Sam recognized him.

"By yourself?"

"The other kids are downstairs," Phillip lied.

"I see," said Sam.

No, you don't, thought Phillip bitterly.

"What are you having today?" Sam asked.

Phillip always ordered a bag of chips and a root beer. "The usual," he said.

Sam pressed his cash register. "Fifty cents," said the cash register.

Phillip noticed a box full of candy bars next to the cash register.

"Your total," said the cash register, "is one dollar."

He handed Sam a dollar while he slipped a candy bar into his pocket. He scooped up the chips and root beer and went to his usual table. Phillip watched Sam work with the young woman behind the counter and ring up customer orders.

A sheriff came in. While he waited for his food, he removed his hat. Sam touched a spot on the sheriff's head. Phillip felt the stolen candy bar burning in his pocket. Did they make prisoner uniforms in junior sizes?

Phillip was so caught up in his thoughts that he didn't notice Sam walk over.

"You forgot ketchup," he said, plunking down a half-used bottle.

"Thanks," said Phillip.

Sam sat down.

"Did you see the sheriff?" he asked.

Phillip nodded. "I mean, yes."

"Got a lump on his head courtesy of some bank robber. Says the thief got his start in crime stealing candy bars."

A chip seemed to stick in Phillip's throat. He took a hard swig of root beer.

"Anything you want to talk about?"

Phillip took the candy bar out of his pocket and slid it across the table into Sam's hand.

"How did you know?" Phillip asked.

"I may be blind, but I'm not stupid."

Phillip made a puzzled sound.

"Beverly saw you do it," Sam said.

Phillip glanced over at the counter. Beverly, the young woman who worked with Sam, was scraping mayonnaise out of a jar. If Phillip had been as flexible as Angela the

Amazing Acrobat, he would have kicked himself. Why was he so stupid? He hung his head and rubbed his sore eyes.

"Are you going to turn me in?" Phillip asked.

"Which table is the sheriff at?" Sam replied.

10

When a trapeze artist falls into the net at the end of the show, he must land flat on his back in the center of the net. Otherwise, he can hurt himself.

Phillip felt like he was falling from a trapeze so high he couldn't even see if there was a net.

"Please don't turn me in," he begged Sam. "I'll make it up."

After a long silence, Sam said, "Okay. How about you answer some questions?"

"About what?"

"About why you ditched school today."

"Ditched?"

"Cut class. Played hooky. Went truant," explained Sam. "What's the reason you aren't in school?"

"I don't know," said Phillip.

"You wouldn't be running away from home, by any chance?"

"Maybe."

"Let me guess. No one understands you. You feel different."

"Are you making fun of me?"

"It's natural for a new kid to feel he doesn't fit in."

"You don't understand," said Phillip. "I'm not just a new kid. I really am different."

"Okay, I'll bite. How are you different?"

"Before I came to Hardingtown, my life was a two-ring circus."

"You mean a three-ring circus," said Sam. "The expression is: 'My life is like a three-ring circus.'"

"No, I really mean it. Two rings. The Windy Van Hooten Circus is a two-ring circus."

"For real?"

"For real," said Phillip. "My parents are circus people."

"Awesome," said Sam.

Phillip leaned in and raised his voice a measured notch.

"You don't understand," Phillip said. "My dad is Leo Laugh-a-Lot. He wears a rainbow wig and a flower pin that squirts water. His signature gag is trying to stuff more than six clowns into a telephone booth. They never fit."

"That's funny," said Sam.

"No, it's not. Know what else? My mom is the fat lady. Not *a* fat lady, *the* fat lady. She wears polka-dot dresses as big as tents. Her neck is thicker than my waist. Do you know how much you have to weigh to be the fat lady at the circus?"

"How much?" said Sam, waiting for the punch line.

"It's not a joke. They call our family the Stupendous Stanislaws," he concluded miserably.

"Let me get this straight," Sam said. "Instead of working boring jobs like my parents, your folks are in show business. Your dad laughs and plays all day, and your mom gets paid for sitting and eating goodies?" Sam raised his shoulders and spread his arms out. "You don't think that's cool?"

"If coming from a circus family is so cool, why did B.B.'s friends laugh at me?"

"Because they don't know what cool is," said Sam.

"That's not the worst of it," Phillip said.

"What is?"

"Dodgeball," said Phillip. "Dodgeball is the worst."

"You mean the game?"

"It's not a game. It's target practice for B.B. Tyson."

"The same B.B. whose friends laughed at you?"

"She's the reason I got this," Phillip said. He held up his bandaged wrist.

"Got what?" asked Sam.

"I sprained my wrist yesterday. Playing dodgeball. B.B. hit Shawn O'Malley, who fell on me, and I sprained my wrist."

"Then you don't have to worry about dodgeball," said Sam. "If you have a sprained wrist you won't be able to play for two or three weeks."

"I never thought of that."

"Sure. Have the school nurse write you a note."

"What do I do after that?"

"Let's worry about that in two or three weeks."

"Okay," agreed Phillip.

He finished his bag of chips and crinkled the bag.

"Here, give it to me," said Sam. "Watch this."

Sam shot the crumpled paper into a corner, where it landed dead center into an open trash can.

"Sam," said Phillip, "I'm sorry about the candy bar."

"I know," said Sam. He went back to the counter, where a man with an expandable folder was waiting on a Dodgeballburger.

The next gym class, Phillip handed Coach the nurse's note

and climbed to the top of the bleachers. Made to watch the other kids get hit, he wasn't alone for long. A thin girl with a red face huffed her way up next to him. Slowly they were joined by others still feeling the sting of the ball.

On the floor, two of the tough kids were battling like they were firing grenades. One of them raced from a screamer smack into the wall. Coach stopped the game to make sure the boy was still alive, then had Shawn O'Malley help him to the bleachers.

"You should go to the nurse's office," Phillip said.

"Shut up," said the tough guy, still teetering as he sat.

"It's not right," Phillip said.

"What?" asked Shawn.

"Kids shouldn't be allowed to purposely hit each other. Somebody ought to do something."

"That'll be the day," said Shawn.

"Dream on," said the girl with the red face.

"You'll get used to it," a boy holding his side explained to Phillip. "That's all you can do."

Phillip didn't want to get used to it. It's not fair, he thought. Whenever something happened in the circus that seemed unfair, he would talk about it with his mom. If it was important enough, she would discuss it with the other circus performers. Then they would hold a circus meeting to debate and vote on a solution. If the vote was a tie, the governor of the circus would make the decision. Whether it was the wrong kind of net for a dangerous stunt or a bigger lion picking on a smaller one, at least somebody tried to resolve the problem.

Unfairness had always made Phillip sick to his stomach. At dinner that night, he had no appetite. By lunch the next day, he still wasn't hungry. Phillip went to clean his locker. Two boys saw him and raced over.

"Hey, did you hear what happened?" asked one.

"A couple of stampeding elephants escaped from a traveling circus," explained the other. Phillip dropped his math book. Stampeding elephants could crush cars, knock down buildings, trample people, not to mention the poop problems.

"Yeah," said the first kid. "The cops found them in the public swimming pool with their trunks down." The boys laughed.

"Get it? Elephant trunks, swim trunks. With their *trunks* down," said one.

"You should have seen the expression on your face," said the other.

Phillip watched them gallop down the hallway, punching each other's arms until they disappeared around a corner. He picked up his math book and returned it to his locker, wondering if he still even wanted to be a "regular" boy. Then he grabbed a bunch of papers from the top shelf and began sorting.

"What grade are you in?" asked a girl who had crept up behind him. It was Carmen, a tanned-skin, dark-haired sixth-grader, wearing stylish black jeans and a glittery shirt. She was one of B.B.'s friends. Why was she talking to him?

"I'm in sixth," he answered.

"Good. Then you can sign this," she told him, holding out a paper on a clipboard and a strawberry-scented pen.

"What is it?" he asked.

"A petition."

"What's a petition?"

"How can you not know what a petition is? What was your job at the circus? Court jester?"

"Court jesters," Phillip said, "are medieval entertainers."

"Whatever," she said, flipping back her thick, wavy locks. "Look, do you want ice cream in the cafeteria?"

"I guess," he said.

"Then sign this."

Phillip took the clipboard and began to read. It said:

We, the undersigned members of the student body of the Hardingtown Middle School, hereby petition the school to serve *ice cream* **in the cafeteria.**

The form was typed, except the part about serving ice cream, which was written in long hand. Underneath it was line after line of student signatures.

"You mean if I sign this, the school will start serving ice cream?"

"Don't be a moron," the girl said, taking the signed paper back from him. "I need to collect one hundred signatures before I can turn it in to the office."

Phillip thought about kids sitting in the cafeteria licking double-dip ice-cream cones, all because of the petition he signed. After school, at the courthouse, he told Sam about it.

"Can anyone petition to change anything at school?" asked Sam.

"I guess," said Phillip.

"What about dodgeball?"

"You can't stop dodgeball with a piece of paper," said Phillip.

"Maybe not stop it completely," Sam said. "But you could petition for a second sport option for kids who don't like dodgeball."

"I don't know," said Phillip. Hadn't he already stirred up enough trouble? Wasn't it better to keep quiet if you wanted to fit in?

"I'll bet plenty of kids dislike playing dodgeball as much as you," said Sam. "It would mean a lot to them."

Phillip knew scads of kids who didn't like dodgeball. The bleachers were full of them at game's end. It would feel great if he could do something to help those kids.

"But why me?" asked Phillip.

"Don't ask yourself why it should be you," said Sam. "Ask yourself why it shouldn't."

Phillip thought about it. If Carmen could petition about ice cream, why couldn't he petition about dodgeball? Then he remembered why. Phillip could see B.B. and her gang closing in on him with their dodgeballs cocked and ready to fire.

"B.B. Tyson will kill me if she finds out I'm petitioning against her favorite sport," he said.

"You don't know, do you?" asked Sam.

Phillip played with the pull tab on his soda-pop can. "Know what?" he asked.

"There's a story they tell in Hardingtown," said Sam. "An old but true story, about an overweight girl who was lonely and wanted to make friends." Sam settled back in his chair and crossed his arms. Phillip leaned in to listen.

"She wanted to try out for the dodgeball team," Sam continued. "But she was overweight; she was an easy target. So she tried out for the Dodgeball Cheerleading Squad instead.

At first, they laughed because she was too fat. But she was so incredibly strong she could easily toss the lighter cheerleaders up."

Phillip could see a picture in his mind of thin young girls sailing through the air in tiny skirts and tights. It reminded him of the circus.

"They made her a base," Sam said. "That's the person on the bottom who holds the other cheerleaders up."

"Did she make friends?" asked Phillip.

"Some," said Sam. "But there was this kid—Stinky. He was captain of the school dodgeball team, the Hardingtown Hedgehogs. He liked to embarrass her in front of the other kids."

"What does this have to do with the petition idea?" asked Phillip.

"Hear me out," said Sam. "On the day of the Regional High School Championship, Stinky was having a bad game. The Hedgehogs had lost one their best players. The cheerleaders began doing a special routine to cheer them up.

"They built a pyramid so high the girl on top looked like she could touch the ceiling. The base was holding it practically by herself. Nobody knew what came over Stinky. One minute, he was standing there holding a dodgeball. The next minute, he was lobbing it at the base of the pyramid."

"What happened?" Phillip asked.

"It collapsed. The cheerleaders came crashing down. Fortunately for them, the Hedgehogs were directly below to help break their fall."

"Not so fortunate for the Hedgehogs," Phillip said.

"That's right," said Sam. "Put the whole team out of commission. They had to forfeit the game. Ended in second place. It was the worst fiasco in Hardingtown dodgeball history."

"That's awful," said Phillip.

Sam nodded his head, slowly. "It wasn't her fault," Sam said, "but they blamed the base cheerleader anyway. A hundred people must have seen Stinky throw that ball, but none of them had the nerve to speak against him. That's how it is with bullies."

Phillip could feel the punch as the ball slammed into the base cheerleader. He could hear the crowd shouting at her, and taste her salty tears as they slipped down her flushed cheeks onto her trembling lips.

"You aren't the first kid in Hardingtown to get picked on by a dodgeball bully," said Sam. "But if you start a petition, you'll be the first kid around here to do something about it."

Phillip nodded. Sam was right. He had to try to help the other dodgeball targets. If enough kids signed the petition, they wouldn't have to worry about dodgeball anymore.

"I'll get a hundred signatures, same as the ice-cream petition," said Phillip.

"Figure out who the biggest dodgeball targets are and talk to them first," Sam advised. "The more signatures you get, the more people will sign. People like to follow the leader." Sam stood and offered Phillip his hand. Phillip shook it. It felt good to have a plan.

The next day, Phillip quickly realized his first signature would be the hardest. After considering a half dozen kids, he decided to ask Shawn, since they sort of had a relationship.

Phillip reasoned with Shawn as Sam had told him to. "Since dodgeball is won by eliminating as many people as possible, the majority are losers. If all the losers get together, we can make them offer us an alternative sport."

"I'll think about it," said Shawn.

"Please," Phillip begged. "I need your help."

"Why should I get involved?" Shawn asked.

"Because if you sign the petition," Phillip said, trying to find a way to appeal to the big boy, "I'll give you my lunch."

It worked. He had his first signature. Phillip looked around. Who would sign next? He saw Carmen. He went over to her lunch table and stood next to her, but she acted like she didn't see him. When she finally stood up to put her tray away, he made his move.

"What do you want?" she said.

"Will you sign my petition?" he asked, presenting it.

"You're standing in my way," she said.

"It's to make dodgeball optional."

"Who died and put you in charge?"

"I'm not in charge. I'm only trying to help."

"Why would I want to sign your petition?"

"I signed yours," he said.

"Mine was important."

"This is important," he said. "There are other sports we could play where kids wouldn't get hurt."

She looked at him for a moment with a serious expression, as if she were thinking it over.

"Let me see the petition," she said.

Phillip held his breath. If she signed, her friends would, too. Carmen took the petition and ran her finger down the page.

"Aha!" she said.

"What?"

"I can't sign this."

"Why not?"

"It hasn't been approved by the student council yet."

"The what?"

"The students we elected to represent us."

"Oh, the student council."

"You can't circulate a petition until the student council clears it. You need a seal in this space down here."

Phillip saw the empty space at the bottom of the form.

"How do I get the student council to approve it?"

"Look," she said, "see that girl in the green sweater?" She pointed to a water fountain where a group of kids were crowded. Phillip could see a piece of the green sweater near the front of the line.

"She's president of the student council," Carmen said. "Go ask her."

Phillip made his way to the girl. She was drinking.

"Excuse me," he said.

The girl stopped and looked up at him. It was B.B. Tyson.

11

Most people think clowns are disorganized. But in each circus there is one clown who is the boss clown. The boss clown is in charge of the other clowns. You can't even pull a rubber chicken out of your pants unless the boss clown approves.

If the Hardingtown Middle School was a circus, B.B. Tyson would be boss clown.

"What do you want?" B.B. demanded when Phillip tapped her shoulder.

Oh no, thought Phillip, wincing inside.

"Are you the president of student council?" he asked.

"Of course I am," she said.

Phillip felt like his stilt had hit deep mud. It seemed hopeless to ask B.B. He had to force the words out.

"I want the student council to approve my petition," he said.

She looked at him suspiciously.

"Is this like your stupid 'hall monitor' joke, Stanislaw?"

"No," he said, mustering his courage. "I want you to approve my petition." He handed her the paper. "It's to give kids an option to play a sport other than dodgeball in gym."

B.B. laughed.

"Are all circus boys chickens like you?" she asked. A small group of kids gathered.

"I'm not a chicken. I don't think it's fair they make us play dodgeball every gym class, that's all," said Phillip.

"The reason you don't like dodgeball is you're afraid of the ball," said B.B. "You're a big, yellow chicken, Stanislaw." B.B. made squawking sounds. She bent her elbows and put her hands under her arms, flapping them in mock chicken motions. Snickers rose around them and grew into full-pitched laughs. Phillip felt his ears turn into thermometers about to burst.

"No," he yelled. "That's not why."

The laughter screeched to a halt. All eyes were on him. He completely forgot he was yelling at someone who could punch his lights out.

"The reason I think dodgeball should be optional," insisted Phillip, "is because I think it's wrong to encourage bigger, stronger kids to hurt smaller, weaker kids."

"Dodgeball is a sport," said B.B. "Kids get hurt playing all kinds of sports. Only sissies whine about it."

"Dodgeball's not a sport. It's target practice for bullies."

"Targets smargets. You're complaining because you're a wimp."

"I am not."

"Then prove it. You and I, one-on-one dodgeball. After school. In the gymnasium. If you win, I'll make the student council approve your stupid petition."

"What happens if I lose?" he asked.

"If you lose . . ." began B.B., scheming a horrible fate for Phillip. "If you lose, you have to change your name from Stanislaw to Coleslaw for the rest of the year."

"Why coleslaw?" asked a boy from the crowd.

"Because nobody likes coleslaw," B.B. said, then turned and tromped off.

Once Phillip calmed down, he was shocked at what he had gotten into. He ran to grab his history book before heading to class. As soon as he got there, Phillip caught a boy whispering and pointing at him. He pretended it was just another school day, but he kept dropping things and couldn't get any answers right. All he could think about was the one-on-one dodgeball game with B.B.

Finally, he asked to go to the bathroom. He wandered down the deserted hallway, and walked past the door that said BOYS. Then he sneaked out the back door of the school and slunk to the courthouse.

As soon as he got to the courthouse, he began to feel he had made a mistake. On the gym floor B.B. would have beaten him, but if he had faced off with her, at least he would have been doing something. That evening, a faint smell like rotting cabbage hung in the air.

The next school day, it took all the nerve Phillip had just to get out of bed. He expected everyone at school to make fun of him. He expected there to be a banner hanging across the face of the Hardingtown Middle School that said:

PHILLIP EDWARD COLESLAW IS A YELLOW-CHICKEN, ELEPHANT-POOP-SCOOPING CIRCUS BOY SISSY.

There wasn't.

He expected kids to laugh when he walked by.

They didn't.

A few kids called him Coleslaw, but most simply avoided

him. Phillip poured himself into his work. The next few weeks passed without incident. Whenever he saw B.B., she glared triumphantly and her friends snickered. There was no way the student council would approve his petition now. There was no use even trying.

Then it happened.

"Stanislaw," Coach called to Phillip as he made his way up the bleachers. "Three weeks is up. You're on the floor today."

Panic filled him.

B.B. dribbled a dodgeball and gave him a menacing wink. Coach mixed things up by picking captains and having them select their teammates. B.B. made sure she didn't pick Phillip for her team. Phillip crept to his side of the gym with a couple of kids anxious to share their dodgeball strategies.

"If you flex your stomach muscles right before the ball hits you, you'll hardly feel it," a student tipped him off.

"Personally," said another, "I'll take a head shot anytime." She knocked on her skull. "It's one of the good things about being hardheaded."

"Stomach shot, head shot, they both have their advantages under the right conditions," said a third, "but overall, I prefer the twisted-shoulder defense."

"What's that?" asked Phillip.

"When you see the ball coming," the kid explained, "you twist your torso so that you take the hit in the square of your top arm. It's the best place to absorb the impact."

Phillip considered his options. He didn't want to climb the rope or hide behind other players. He was tired of running away. They are not custard pies, he reminded himself. They are balls. How much could a dodgeball hurt?

Seeing one coming, he held still and waited for impact. It

whizzed past, so close he could taste its stiff, inflatable rubber. The gym floor vibrated faintly as kids ran and dodged and fell against it. Screams, laughs, and grunts filled Phillip's ears as balls found their marks. But he did not move.

"This is for you, Coleslaw," he heard B.B. yell. The burning ball sped at him like a meteor racing toward Earth, anxious to form a nasty crater.

Defiantly, he closed his eyes.

WHAP!!!! The ball pounded him on the side of the head at the temple. His glasses dug across his nose. They flew off and sailed across the room, crashing against a wall. Phillip held his burning face in his hands and struggled to keep from crying.

Coach blew his whistle and stopped the game. Phillip located the pieces of his glasses and made his way to the bleachers, where he sat with the other defeated players.

"You should have tried the twisted-shoulder defense," one said.

Phillip examined his glasses. In one hand, he held the scratched lenses; in the other, the bent metal frames. Without his glasses on, Phillip was lucky he could even find his way to the courthouse after school. Twice he went down the wrong street and had to turn around.

"Dodgeball?" Aunt Veola asked when she saw his bruised nose. Phillip nodded and handed her the broken glasses.

"Uncle Felix can fix them," she said. "He worked at an optical shop. One time he forgets to lock the door and, wouldn't you know, burglars took all the inventory."

When they got home, Uncle Felix used a pair of pliers to straighten out the twisted metal.

"It's all a matter of holding the frames while you twist back with the pliers," Uncle Felix said.

Crack! The left earpiece snapped off.

"Or was it a matter of holding the pliers while you twist back with the frames?"

Uncle Felix used a piece of red electrical tape to reattach the earpiece. He forced the plastic lenses back into the mangled frames and carefully set the glasses on Phillip's nose.

Plop! The right lens fell out.

Uncle Felix put the right lens back in and used the electrical tape to secure it to the metal of the frame. When he placed them back on Phillip's nose, the only place to see through was a peephole in the middle.

"You've got more red tape here than city hall," said the lady at the optical shop as she unwrapped Uncle Felix's handiwork to evaluate the damage. "Better look for a new pair of frames. These are beyond repair. We'll have to replace the lenses, too."

When she gave them a price for the new glasses, Aunt Veola exclaimed, "Two hundred and forty-nine dollars! You can buy a lawn mower for two hundred and forty-nine dollars."

"True," said the optical lady, "but he won't be able to see a blackboard with a lawn mower on his nose." Aunt Veola reached for her checkbook.

"Do I have to pay it all up front?" she asked.

"I'll need at least fifty dollars down," said the lady.

Phillip squirmed. He wished he could tell Aunt Veola not to bother, that he could do without his glasses. The optical lady began filling out a form.

"I'll find a way to pay you back," Phillip told Aunt Veola. "I promise I will." It didn't seem fair that Aunt Veola had to pay for his new glasses because B.B. Tyson broke his old pair. On purpose.

The optical lady finished the paperwork and said, "It will take three or four weeks to get them."

Phillip was as disappointed as a ticket holder to a canceled show. He picked up the broken glasses and began rewrapping them.

The next day at school, he tried to hunch slightly and walk with his head toward the wall. But it was hopeless.

"Nice look, Coleslaw," teased a boy.

"You should have tried the back block," said a girl.

B.B. and Carmen spotted him going into science class. "You look like a clown," said Carmen. "Why don't you go back to the circus?"

"Beat it," B.B. told Carmen. "I want to talk to him alone." As Carmen slithered off, Phillip felt a shudder run through him.

"It's about your glasses, Coleslaw. I—"

"What's going on?" asked Coach, who was suddenly behind them.

"Nothing, Daddy," said B.B.

"Then you'd better get to class," he said.

In science class, Phillip kept hearing B.B.'s friend telling him to go back to the circus. Miss Castapio was talking about the Periodic Table of Elements, but Phillip wasn't paying attention. Lulled by her hypnotic voice, his mind wandered back to his circus days.

"Mr. Stanislaw," called a woman's voice. "I'm talking to you, Mr. Stanislaw." It was Miss Castapio.

Phillip shook his head to bring himself back. The kids laughed.

"Didn't you hear the message on the loudspeaker?" she said. "You're wanted in the vice-principal's office."

12

It's difficult for a human cannonball to keep his cool while waiting to get blasted over a crowd of spectators. The temperature is hotter when you're crammed inside a circus cannon.

The waiting area outside Hardingtown Middle School's vice-principal's office had the reverse problem—it was too cold. The students said that the vice-principal, Mr. Race, kept it that way on purpose because it had the effect of slowing down a student's body. Many an angry hothead had been reduced to a shivering pile of goose bumps by the time it was his or her turn to go in. Legend had it that a particularly troublesome student had to wait so long he got frostbite and transferred to another school district. Phillip cupped his hands and blew into them.

The walls outside the vice-principal's office were concrete block painted an odd yellow, like brown mustard. On one wall, a poster said: THE PRINCIPAL IS YOUR PAL. Phillip sat on his hands to keep them warm. As the dismissal bell rang, he thought about the sweatshirt that was hanging in his locker. After twenty minutes passed, the vice-principal's secretary appeared.

"You can go wait in his office," she said. "He'll be right in."

The vice-principal's office was as clean as a knife-thrower's blade. Phillip sat in one of the stiff vinyl chairs in front of the metal desk. On the desk was an IN box and an OUT box, both empty. On his teachers' desks, Phillip had noticed brightly colored knickknacks. There was nothing bright on the vice-principal's desk. It was as if vibrant colors were banned from his office, replaced by creams and grays and browns, colors that wouldn't cause a commotion. That's what the secretary had told Phillip that the vice-principal wanted to see him about—causing a commotion.

Mr. Race blew by him and plopped into his swiveling seat. The musky, aftershave-scented breeze made the flesh stand up on the back of Phillip's neck. Mr. Race wore shiny braces on his not quite perfect teeth. His medium brown hair was parted down the middle with such accuracy that Phillip imagined there were exactly the same number of hairs on each side of his head. Mr. Race was always in a hurry. His name suited him.

Mr. Race opened a thin folder that was on his desk.

"Phillip Edward Stanislaw. Grade six," he read.

While Mr. Race read from his school file, Phillip stared at the collection of antique handcuffs in the display case behind the desk. There was also a small dodgeball trophy. The gold plate on it said: SECOND PLACE.

A knock rattled the door.

"She's here," said his secretary, pushing the door open.

Phillip turned and saw Aunt Veola in her courthouse-guard uniform. She removed a fresh handkerchief from her pocket and wiped her hand with it.

"Thank you for coming, Veola," said Mr. Race as they shook hands. Aunt Veola discreetly wiped her hand again and sat next to Phillip.

"We are both busy people, Veola. I hope you don't mind if I get straight to it."

"No need for dawdling," she agreed.

"We are suspending your nephew," Mr. Race said. "We have a rule against circulating petitions without the approval of student council. He violated that rule." Aunt Veola looked at Phillip, who sat wide-eyed and speechless.

"I didn't know," Phillip said.

Mr. Race opened a desk drawer and removed a petition form. He flipped it over and read out loud, "'All petitions must be approved by student council before they may be circulated.'"

"Now, Veola," continued Mr. Race. "You're a law-abiding citizen, so you understand that we can't allow students to break our rules without punishment."

"They have to obey the rules," Aunt Veola agreed. "But suspension—even for a short time—isn't that a bit harsh?"

"A four-day out-of-school suspension will give the boy a chance to think about his transgression."

"You're not going extra hard on him because of what happened between you and my sister when you were in school together?"

"Of course not," insisted Mr. Race.

"Because it wouldn't be right to punish him just because he's Matilda's son."

Phillip wondered what they were talking about.

Mr. Race smiled, and a glint of light reflected off his

braces. "I might take a different approach if this were Phillip's first offense," he continued, "but there have been others."

"Others?" asked Aunt Veola.

"He's left school early without permission on two occasions. The first time was an early morning; he was spotted in the hallway but failed to report to homeroom. The second time, he asked to go to the bathroom and never returned to class. Of course there are also complaints about his bad dodgeball attitude. I'm sure you understand how important school spirit is."

"He's had a hard time adjusting," Aunt Veola said weakly.

"Attacking dodgeball is not my idea of trying to adjust." Mr. Race looked over at Phillip. "If you really want to adjust, start with your attitude."

"What's the difference?" Phillip replied. "I'll never fit in."

They did not discuss the point further. Phillip collected his schoolbooks and loaded them into Aunt Veola's car. He held his feelings in for as long as he could. By the time they were driving away from the school, he was filled to the brim and began to overflow.

"I'm no good at anything," he said. "When I was with the circus, I wasn't brave enough to walk on hot coals, patient enough to train a bear to dance, or graceful enough to stand on a horse. I thought if I lived like a regular kid, I would find a place where I belong. But things are no better here."

Phillip sighed. "I'm not strong enough to be an athlete. I'm not rich enough to be a snob. Even the nerds don't want me because I'm not nerdy enough."

"It takes all types in this world," said Aunt Veola. "Not

everyone is an athlete or a snob or a nerd. Just look at your father, and he's a very successful clown."

"But clowning comes easy to him. He's always been a clown."

"Is that what you think?" Aunt Veola pulled over to the side of the road, waited for traffic, and made a U-turn. Phillip didn't care. Nothing seemed to matter.

The sedan didn't stop until the scenery had turned to countryside. They pulled into the parking lot of a run-down country diner. Phillip followed Aunt Veola to a pickup window. She ordered two hot chocolates with extra whipped cream and put her change in a tin box on the counter for donations to the Dodgeball Museum.

Aunt Veola wiped her cup with a paper napkin. They took the cups to a large pond and watched a family of ducks diving for dinner. October leaves were blowing in swirling patterns. Aunt Veola spread a napkin on a wooden bench, where they sipped their rich, soothing drinks.

"I used to fish here with your mother when we were girls. I would catch them. She would eat them."

Phillip tried to imagine Aunt Veola as a young girl with a fishing rod in her hand and a can of disinfectant in her pocket to clean the hook between worms.

"After your mother joined the circus," she said, "I stopped fishing. I sold my rod and reel the day of her wedding. I knew she would never move back after she became one of the Stupendous Stanislaws."

Phillip listened with interest. He sipped his hot chocolate slowly, letting it clear a warm path down his throat.

"You don't know much about your father's family history. Do you?" she asked.

Phillip shook his head.

"Your great-grandparents on your father's side of the family were turnip farmers. They were sensible people, hoping to raise your grandfather to be a sensible man. They taught him that 'the early bird catches the worm' and 'a penny saved is a penny earned.' They took him to turnip-farming conventions and bought him books about crop rotation and soil conditions.

"One day your grandfather was riding in the back of the truck on the way to market with a load of turnips. They hit a bump in the road, and your grandfather fell off the turnip truck. In the distance, he saw a circus tent. It was your grandfather's eighteenth birthday. He looked at his parents' turnip truck rumbling down the dusty road. He looked at the colorful tent. Your grandfather got the last ticket for the afternoon show. There he fell in love at first sight with the lion tamer's daughter."

Phillip guessed, "Grandma Maybell?"

"That's right," said Aunt Veola. "He joined the circus, and they got married. Your grandfather became one of the greatest lion tamers in circus history. Then your father was born. They named him after the fiercest lion in the act."

"Leo Laugh-a-Lot?" asked Phillip.

"Back then," Aunt Veola explained, "his name was Leo the Ferocious. More than anything else in the world, he wanted to be a great lion tamer like his father."

Phillip asked, "Why didn't he?"

"It turned out he was allergic. His sneezing and wheezing got so bad that one day, when he was eleven, his parents sent him to live with relatives in Arizona."

"I didn't know," said Phillip.

"It's not something he talks about. The fact is, he was miserable. The circus was in his blood. When he turned eighteen, he came back and took up clowning."

"What happened to his allergies?"

"He had outgrown them," she said. "The day he went back, he met your mother, who had joined the circus the year before. She was juggling flaming arrows. They fell in love and got married. Then you came along. They were so happy. Your father swore he would be a clown forever, and he would never leave the circus again."

Phillip looked down at his half-full cup of hot chocolate. The steam was gone, but it still tasted good.

"We each have a place in this world," Aunt Veola said. "Someday, you'll find out where you belong. Do you understand?"

Phillip nodded.

"Until that day comes," she added, "you need to stay out of trouble."

A unicyclist trying to ride on a high wire can use an umbrella to maintain his balance. An eleven-year-old boy trying to avoid trouble on a four-day suspension from school is on his own.

The next morning, Phillip accompanied Aunt Veola to the courthouse. He sat in a wooden chair next to the metal detector, counting floor tiles and thinking about his visit to the vice-principal's office.

"You're not going extra hard on him because of what happened between you and my sister when you were in school together?" Aunt Veola had asked Mr. Race. After Phillip had counted all the floor tiles, out loud, twice, he asked Aunt Veola what she meant.

"Some parts of a person's past are better left in the past," she said.

A short, old man with a long, white beard made the metal detector go off as he passed through. Aunt Veola swept her handheld device under his whiskers and made him remove a tiny flag pin from his shirt collar.

"But I still want to know," said Phillip.

Aunt Veola watched a tiny television-like screen showing

an X-ray picture of the items in the man's bag.

"Please?" Phillip asked.

She stared at the screen a long time before she spoke.

"Someday, when the time is right, we'll talk about it."

Before Phillip could ask another question, she removed a crisp five-dollar bill from her billfold, let it drop into his hand, and sent him to the snack bar.

Phillip realized that if he went to the snack bar Sam would ask him why he wasn't in school. What would Sam think when he told him he had gotten suspended? Would Sam still want to be his friend if he knew how much trouble he kept getting into? Phillip wasn't in the mood to find out. He looked around for another place to hang out.

He saw a room with comfortable-looking upholstered couches and a nameplate that read: LAWYERS' LOUNGE. Ancient men in dark business suits sat in thick leather chairs reading newspapers and napping. Scattered about were end tables of decorative wrought iron that were topped with sheets of clear, thin glass. Phillip kept looking.

On the fourth floor, he saw a sign: LAW LIBRARY. Perfect, he thought. As Phillip entered the library, he could smell musty, aging books. The bookcases went from floor to ceiling, with a stepladder at the end of each row. The tables were heavy oak with matching chairs that made clunky sounds when moved. No one was sleeping here. Men and women were busy searching shelves.

A young lawyer with a yellow notepad strode down an aisle and examined a row of books. She grabbed a volume and retreated to a table. Phillip inspected the hole she left. Each one of the books around it was precisely the same size, shape, and color. Only the small numbers on the books differed: Atlantic 2nd. 487, Atlantic 2nd. 488, Atlantic 2nd. 489. Phillip thought maybe the books were about oceans. He slid one off the shelf and looked through it. The words appeared to be English, but they didn't make any sense. "Discovery rule tolls statute of limitations," he read. Phillip slipped the book back into its hole.

Wandering into the next aisle, he found more sets of matching volumes. He passed through row after row, occasionally pulling a volume and examining it. The print in each book was so tiny and the pages so numerous that Phillip believed he could empty his entire brain and not fill even one volume.

At the far end, the bookcases were lower, covering only three-fourths of the wall. A small, bright green book sitting on the highest shelf caught his eye, but he was too short to reach it. Phillip stepped onto the first shelf. He was almost there. He stepped onto the second shelf.

Suddenly, he felt the bookcase begin to wobble. As Phillip jumped off, the bookcase gave way. It crashed down, spewing books onto him.

"Ahhhhhhh!" he screamed.

Phillip expected to feel the hefty, wooden bookcase flatten him like a cardboard clown run over by a steamroller. But the bookcase did not hit him. Its top was wedged against one of the tall units standing firmly behind him.

Rescuers dug him out, then chewed him out for being there. Once the law librarian, Mr. Chang, determined that Phillip was not injured and that the boy was Veola's trouble-making nephew, he issued a proclamation.

"Young man," Mr. Chang said to Phillip, "you are not leaving here until you have picked up these books and properly reshelved them."

A couple of strong men in suits lifted the bookcase and righted it, mumbling about faulty shelving and product liability lawsuits. Phillip picked up the books, methodically—one at a time—and put them back on the shelves.

After a while, he found the green book that had caught his attention. Its title was *Fighting Back in Court*. Phillip opened the book. On the first page, a lawyer wrote about how the book would teach people their legal rights and how to file their own lawsuits.

Phillip knew what a lawsuit was. Even though he wasn't allowed to watch television, he did go to the movies sometimes. Bartholomew the Giant had once taken him to see a movie about a lawsuit. Plus, once the circus hired a lawyer for the purchase of an exotic animal, although it turned out the lawyer didn't know the difference between a double-humped camel and a dromedary.

"So that was Matilda's kid."

"Yep. Spilled the whole load of books." The voices came from the next aisle over. They were hushed but loud enough for Phillip to make out the words.

"Like mother, like son."

"Whatever happened to Matilda?"

"Who knows, and, after what she did, who cares?"

Phillip dropped the green book and tiptoed to the end of his aisle. He peeked around the corner to see who was talking, but they were gone. Why were they making such strange remarks about his mom?

Phillip returned to the green book and kept reading. He learned that purposely hitting someone with an object is called "an assault and battery." If you commit an assault and battery—if you hit someone—and you hurt them or damage their property, you should be held responsible. According to the law, you have to pay that person money to fix the damaged property.

Being careful not to pop the lenses out, Phillip pushed his broken glasses back up his nose. He kept reading, skipping the hard or boring parts. So the librarian wouldn't get mad, he reshelved the fallen books with one hand while he read the green book in the other. By the time Phillip was done shelving the books, he had reached the last chapter, "How to File a Small Claim." Phillip wondered if he should stay out of trouble by leaving alone the matter with B.B. and his glasses, or if he should fight back in court for money to pay back Aunt Veola.

He slid the green book into the bookcase and went into Mr. Chang's cubicle.

"Where do people go when they need legal advice?" he asked Mr. Chang.

"Depends what's in their pockets," said Mr. Chang. "Rich people call the County Bar Association and get a referral to a private attorney. Poor people talk to the public defender."

Phillip pulled one dollar and twenty-five cents from his pocket.

"Where can I find the public defender?" he asked.

Once a circus performance begins, only the death or serious injury of a performer can stop it. Once Phillip decided to find legal help for his broken eyeglasses problem, he wasn't about to let anything stop him.

"Hello," he said to the lady sitting behind the desk in the public defender's office. She had a clump of dark hair piled on top of her head, held by an array of clips and pins, and wore a pink ruffled dress shirt. She scrunched her eyes and frowned as she tapped on a computer keyboard. It took a while before she even noticed Phillip.

"Can I help you?" she finally asked, suspiciously.

"I have legal questions," said Phillip. "I tried to follow along in the book, but it got confusing."

"Are your parents here?" she asked. Phillip shook his head.

"Do you have a guardian?" she asked.

"What's a guardian?"

"If you have to ask, you don't have one," she said, returning to her work. "Come back with your mother or father."

"My mom and dad don't live here," Phillip said.

"Then who do you stay with?"

"My Aunt Veola and Uncle Felix."

"You said you didn't have a guardian," she huffed.

"No, *you* said I didn't."

"Are you getting smart with me?" she asked, with a raised voice. Phillip shook his head.

"Come back with your aunt or uncle," she said.

"But they're busy at work."

"So am I."

Phillip felt his ears heating up. Aunt Veola could explain about his parents not being there, but he couldn't ask her to come to the public defender's office until her shift was over. By then, the office might be closed.

He checked the clock on the woman's desk. It was a novelty clock. On the ends of the hour and minute hands were silhouettes of running children. On the end of the second hand was a dodgeball. When the second hand swept by the hour hand, he could almost hear Coach yell, "You're out."

"Don't just stand there," she said. "Go on now."

He gritted his teeth. "I want to talk to a lawyer."

She gave a mean face.

"Listen, boy," she said, "if you don't get out of here, I'm going to call security."

A picture flashed in Phillip's mind of Aunt Veola rushing up the steps and bursting into the room.

"Please do," he said. If Aunt Veola did come, he would be allowed to see the lawyer.

The mean-faced lady stared angrily. Phillip stared back. It reminded him of one of his dad's routines. Two clowns staring each other down over some silliness. He half expected her to pull out a seltzer bottle and spray him.

Bzzzzz.

The phone made a strange noise, and the sound of a woman's voice came out.

"What's all the commotion out there?" the voice from the telephone intercom said. "I'm trying to write a brief."

The mean-faced lady picked up the phone.

"Not to worry, Ms. Johnson," said Mean Face to the receiver. "It's only a boy."

Mean Face paused.

"I'll ask him," she said. Mean Face covered the receiver and said dryly, "She wants to know what you want."

"I want to talk to a lawyer," said Phillip.

"He wants to talk to a lawyer," said Mean Face to Ms. Johnson. "I told him he needs a parent, but he refuses to leave."

Phillip wondered if he had really refused to leave.

"She said to send you back," said Mean Face. "She'd like to take a look at this troublemaker."

Phillip gulped.

Mean Face pointed down a dimly lit hallway.

He stopped at a half-opened door that said: MS. DAISY JOHNSON, ESQ., ASSISTANT PUBLIC DEFENDER. She had a friendly name. But Phillip knew that things weren't always what they seemed. After all, the most bloodthirsty animal in the circus is the human flea.

"Don't lurk in the hallway," Ms. Johnson said. Phillip pushed the heavy door open.

"Come in and have a seat." She was a pretty blond woman, wearing a flowery dress and chewing bubble gum. Her desk was covered with wrinkled papers and upside-down books.

Phillip sat in a worn, overstuffed chair.

"You have a legal problem?" she guessed.

He nodded.

"I have an appointment in ten minutes," she said. "So you'll have to talk fast."

Phillip didn't know where to begin. He couldn't tell her everything in ten minutes. It took his dad longer than that to put on his makeup.

"B.B. Tyson won't stop trying to hit me," Phillip said.

"I take it this B.B. Tyson is a school bully. Is that how your glasses got broken?" she asked.

He nodded again.

"If a bully is beating you up, that's a juvenile-crime matter," she said.

"She's not beating me up," Phillip explained. "She's hitting me with a dodgeball. In gym class."

"You mean playing dodgeball? I can't make a criminal case out of two kids playing." She leaned back in her seat and blew a fruity-fresh bubble.

"But it said in this law book that if you intentionally hit someone and you hurt them, you have to pay for their damages."

"That's true," she said. "The civil law does say that."

Phillip gave her a confused look. She took the gum out and held it while she explained.

"There are two kinds of law in this country: criminal and civil. Criminal law applies when people commit crimes and have to go to jail. Civil law is for when they damage other people's property and have to pay money to fix it." She popped the gum back in.

"I want B.B. to pay money damages," said Phillip, "so I can pay back Aunt Veola for my new glasses."

"In a civil action for assault, you would have to prove that B.B. intentionally hit you. Do you think you can prove that?"

Phillip nodded.

"You wouldn't only be putting the bully on trial. You would be putting the whole game of dodgeball on trial." She blew a small bubble and burst it with a loud pop. "I couldn't help you personally. I'm a criminal lawyer and I work for the government. You would have to hire a private lawyer. How much money do you have?"

Phillip dug into his pocket and pulled out his $1.25.

"That wouldn't cover the filing fees," she told him. "Is that it?"

"I get a dollar a day for snack money. I could start saving it," said Phillip.

"Let's be realistic," said Ms. Johnson. She pulled out a long, thin line of gum and twisted it around her finger while she thought. Finally, she said, "You're going to need a civil lawyer who will do your case pro bono."

"Pro who?" Phillip asked.

"Pro bono is Latin. It means 'for the public good.' In other words," she explained, "you need a lawyer who will work for free."

"Lawyers do that?" he asked.

"Some do, depending on the case. You need someone who believes principle is more important than pay. It's got to be someone who is smart and tough and isn't afraid to stand up against the whole town if he has to. There's only one Hardingtown lawyer who would be willing to even consider such a thing. I'll arrange for you to meet him."

In the era before automobiles, a circus would march down the main street. When the parade was to begin, the circus owner, called the governor, would yell to the townspeople, "Hold your horses," so they wouldn't be frightened by the exotic animals. To noncircus people, the expression came to mean "Have patience while you wait for something."

The next day, as Phillip waited for the mystery lawyer, he could hardly hold his horses. Ms. Johnson was supposed to meet Phillip at the snack bar at 2 P.M. and introduce them. Phillip borrowed a law book and took it to the snack bar to study while he waited. The book was full of interesting cases. In each, two people, the plaintiff and the defendant, would tell their story. Then the judge would say who won the case and why.

Phillip was reading about a tavern fight when he saw Sam heading his way. He didn't want to be rude, but he hoped Sam wouldn't want to chat.

Sam sat at his table. "What's up?" he asked.

"The sky," said Phillip.

"I heard about the suspension," Sam said. "Bad break."

"I guess," said Phillip. He looked over Sam's shoulder for the mystery lawyer.

"How's your case coming?" Sam asked.

"You know about that?" asked Phillip.

"Like they say in Disneyland, it's a small world."

Phillip grinned. He filled Sam in on the details of the lawsuit and told him about the meeting.

"Maybe you should leave before the lawyer gets here," said Phillip, trying to be polite. "It's a business meeting."

A man with a suit and tie entered the snack bar and went to the front counter. Phillip strained to see if it was him. Sam went to the counter and took the man's order for an eggsalad sandwich and a cup of coffee to go.

Phillip was disappointed that Sam, and not the importantlooking man, sat back down at his table. After what seemed like a long time, Ms. Johnson came in. She was alone. She headed straight for Phillip's table.

"I see the two of you have met," she said.

"How have you been?" asked Sam as their hands found each other. The handshake lasted a long time.

"I thought you were going to bring the lawyer," Phillip said to Ms. Johnson.

"Didn't he tell you?" she replied. "Sam is the lawyer."

Phillip felt he had misjudged Ms. Johnson. She didn't seem like the kind of person to joke. But she had to be joking. Sam was a cashier. A blind cashier.

"Sam works at the snack bar," Phillip said. "He's not a lawyer."

"Then I guess they'll have to take down that portrait of him at the law school," she said. She blew a grape-scented bubble. It burst like one of his dad's exploding cigars.

Phillip looked at Sam. "Are you a lawyer?" he asked.

"I don't practice anymore," Sam said. "But I still have my license."

"He retired a few years back," explained Ms. Johnson. "He was a pioneer for blind lawyers in his younger days, successfully forcing the state to make them give blind law students special accommodations so they could practice law."

Sam and Ms. Johnson talked about a case that Sam had argued before the United States Supreme Court. They also talked about Sam retiring, and Ms. Johnson kidded him about taking the part-time job at the snack bar because he missed being part of the legal community.

"Are you going to be my lawyer?" Phillip asked Sam.

"I don't know," said Sam. "I have to be selective when I decide whether or not to take a pro bono case."

"Why?"

"Because some clients are quitters," said Sam. "They want you to work for them. But in the end, when the case gets tough, they run away."

Phillip knew what Sam was referring to—the time he left school so he didn't have to play the one-on-one game with B.B. and the time when he decided to run away after B.B. teased him about being a circus boy.

"If you'll be my lawyer on this case," Phillip said, "I won't quit."

"No matter how hard it gets?" Sam asked.

"I promise," said Phillip. "I'm done with running away from my problems."

Sam stood up and extended his hand. Even as Phillip shook it, he wondered if he could live up to his promise.

16

Walking in floppy shoes and breathing through a rubber nose is not as easy as it looks. If you want to be a clown, you need to spend a lot of time in baggy pants.

Phillip knew that if he wanted to sue B.B., it was not going to be easy. He would have to spend a lot of time in the law library. Sam would supervise, but Phillip was to get the papers ready. He found a book about drafting a complaint—the paper that tells a person why you're suing them. The back of the book had fill-in-the-blank forms. Phillip found a form for assault and battery and made a photocopy using his lunch money. He filled in the blank spaces.

Where it said *plaintiff,* he put his name. Where it said *defendant,* he put B.B. Tyson. In the section for what the lawsuit was about, he wrote about his glasses getting broken. For damages, he wrote: *The cost of replacing my glasses because it wasn't Aunt Veola's fault.*

"What are you doing?" asked the librarian, Mr. Chang, who was suddenly looking over his shoulder.

"Nothing," said Phillip, flipping his notepad upside down to cover the complaint.

"You're up to something," Mr. Chang said. He reached over and picked up the notepad.

"It's just a lawsuit," Phillip said as he tried to grab it back.

"Stanislaw versus Tyson," said Mr. Chang. He read the complaint out loud. "Suing the school bully," he observed. "You are either the bravest kid in school or the most stupid."

Phillip shrugged.

"I give you credit. You got guts, kid. Wish I'd thought of it when I was your age." He tossed the complaint back on the table. "Too bad you're wasting your time."

"What do you mean?" Phillip asked.

"I mean," said Mr. Chang, "even if you win, what stops B.B. from doing the same thing next week?"

"I don't know," said Phillip. He hadn't thought about it. Even if he did win his lawsuit and got B.B. to pay for his glasses, it wouldn't stop her from hitting him again.

"What should I do?" asked Phillip.

"Have you heard of the twisted-shoulder block?" asked Mr. Chang. "The shoulder absorbs most of the impact, and you can protect your eyeglasses better." He gave Phillip a pat on the back, wished him good luck, and went back in his cubicle.

Phillip wrestled with what he had said. After lunch he asked Sam about it.

"The only way you could stop it from happening again," said Sam, "is if you got an injunction."

"A what?"

"An injunction," Sam explained, "is like, when your mother yells, *'Knock it off or else!!!'* In a lawsuit, when someone is doing something they're not supposed to do and they keep doing it, the judge can issue an order that says, 'Knock it off or else.'"

"So the judge could order B.B. not to hit me anymore?"

"That's right."

"What about the other kids? Could the judge order them all to stop hitting each other?"

"It's possible," agreed Sam. "But the judge would be ordering an end to school dodgeball. To get a judge to do that, you would need good legal reasoning and plenty of case law on your side."

"I better get back to the library," said Phillip.

Two hours later, he was two hours older and still hadn't a clue as to how he could get a judge to issue an injunction against dodgeball. Phillip wondered how he could have expected to figure all this legal stuff out.

Sheer will was not enough. It was like when Helena took Einstein to the racetrack and tried to train him to race. The elephant lumbered away, always keeping three feet on the ground, while animals with shorter legs easily passed him.

Phillip needed to get away from the musty smell of old books. He left the library and went to the lawyers' lounge, where he found a copy of *Dodgeball Today* magazine on a couch. The lead article was "How to Get More Force on a Screamer Ball Without Making It Explode." Phillip placed the magazine in a rack on the wall. Then he curled up on the couch and fell into a troubled sleep. His nap was interrupted by the chatter of lawyers coming into the lounge. Phillip ignored them and pretended he was asleep.

"Someone beat you to the couch, Syd," a lawyer with a squeaky voice said.

"Looks like Veola's nephew," said a deeper voice. "Almost got himself killed the other day dancing with a bookcase. Fool kid."

"Seems to me," a more soft-spoken voice said, "if you're going to make a bookcase, you ought to make it so it doesn't tip over."

"There he goes," said Deep Voice. "Thinking like a plaintiff's lawyer."

"Yeah," said Squeaky Voice. "I'm surprised you didn't pass the kid your business card."

"Go ahead and laugh," said Soft Spoken. "There's a lawsuit in that bookcase-falling-over mishap. In my opinion, that bookcase was an unreasonably unsafe product."

"No," said Deep Voice, "a product isn't unreasonably unsafe unless it's unsafe for the purpose for which it was made. If you get hurt using a bookcase as a bookcase, it's unreasonably unsafe. If you get hurt using a bookcase as a ladder, you're a fool kid."

The lawyers laughed, but Phillip was thinking about an "unreasonably unsafe product." Wasn't a dodgeball a product? And wasn't the purpose of a dodgeball to hit other kids with? And wasn't it unsafe to hit kids with a dodgeball? Phillip bolted upright.

"Excuse me," he said to the lawyers. He got to his feet and returned to the library.

By the end of the next day, Phillip added a new paragraph to his complaint. It said that a dodgeball was an unreasonably unsafe product, and the judge should issue an injunction to stop the school from forcing kids to play.

Phillip wasn't sure whom to sue about dodgeball being unsafe. He didn't think it was B.B.'s fault. It was Coach and the school that made him play. Since Phillip wanted to be fair, he wrote *Hardingtown Middle School* and *Coach Tyson* next to B.B.'s name as defendants. Then, as a last-minute thought, he added *the American Dodgeball Company* and *the City of Hardingtown*.

Now it was poop-scooping, rope-climbing, broken-glasses sixth-grader Phillip Edward "Coleslaw" Stanislaw (a.k.a. "circus boy") against the Unofficial Dodgeball Capital of the World.

17

Elephant tail hair is considered such a good-luck charm that circus folk braid it into bracelets to wear during performances. As Phillip plodded to school the Tuesday after his suspension and saw his bare wrist, he wished he believed in lucky charms. He could use a bit of good luck.

"Hey, look who's back," said a kid.

"What's up, Coleslaw?" said another.

It was weird. They sounded happy to see him. What was weirder was that Phillip felt happy to be back. Not happy to face another gym class, but happy to see his classmates and teachers and get back to his school subjects.

The rest of the week passed quickly. In English, they worked on declarative sentences. In science, they started projects for the science fair. In history, they learned about the Industrial Revolution.

If only there were no gym class tomorrow, Phillip thought Sunday evening. Another stomachache made him skip dinner. He went to bed early but had trouble falling asleep. When he was a little boy and he couldn't sleep, he and his mom would play war with a deck of magic cards. No matter how they shuffled, they would draw the same cards. Phillip's eyes would droop, and his mom would tuck him in, pulling the covers up around his big ears.

Phillip wished he were little again.

He looked over at his circus trunk, still where he dropped it on his first day in Hardingtown. Wondering if the cards were in it, he slipped out of bed and lifted the trunk latch. It made a familiar creaking sound. Beneath a rubber chicken and whoopee cushion, he found his pogo stick and juggling balls.

He tossed the three balls into the air and mixed them around, letting them drop back onto his black satin cape in the trunk one at a time. Phillip picked up the cape and unfolded it. A white envelope fell out. His name was written across the envelope, in his mom's handwriting. His hands began to perspire as he pulled the flap loose and opened the letter.

Dear Phillip:
I am writing this letter as you pack your bag to go and already I am missing you. We love you and hope you will make lots of friends in public school and be happy. Mind your aunt and uncle and try to remember to eat, even when you're not hungry. If you need us, you can find us on the schedule.

Love,
Mom

There was another paper inside the envelope. It was a schedule of where the Windy Van Hooten Circus would be performing during the year. Phillip scooted back into bed and checked the schedule. The Barlow Street Fairgrounds in

Poughkeepsie, New York. That's where his mom and dad were tonight. He read the schedule from top to bottom, again and again, until he began to doze off.

When he woke the next morning, Phillip devoured a bowl of sugary cereal, three fried eggs, and four pieces of buttered toast. When they counted off at gym class, for the first time, he and B.B. were both "ones."

Phillip adjusted his broken glasses, careful not to pop the lenses, and watched B.B. playing dodgeball from behind. She pushed down and flung up as if in slow motion and caught a ball intent on whizzing past her.

"You're out," Coach screamed at the dejected thrower.

B.B. flung a torpedo ball with such accuracy it sped between two kids standing side by side and grazed both of their arms at the same time.

"You're both out," Coach yelled at the disgraced duo.

Sweat formed on the back of B.B.'s T-shirt as she raced after the balls. She dove and stretched like a trapeze artist. No wonder she was the star of the dodgeball court. She wasn't just a clown throwing pies. She had athletic artistry. He studied her every move. With B.B. on his team, Phillip's side won easily.

During the next gym class, Phillip counted the number of kids forming in the line between him and B.B. and made sure they were an odd number of spaces away. That way, they would be on the same team again. He tried to stay as far from B.B. as he could so she wouldn't realize what he was doing. For the next couple of weeks, his system worked. But even a magician sometimes pulls out the wrong card.

"Two," said B.B, from the front of the line, one afternoon.

"One," said Phillip from the rear.

The game started slow. Three balls were in play. Phillip dodged a low one. Most of the action was on the other side of the gym, where a couple of the better players had gotten into a skirmish near the ball line.

Where was B.B.? He found her and their eyes locked. She had a ball.

"Get the circus boy," a boy with bulging biceps barked.

"Go on. Cream him," shouted another.

B.B. was a statue.

"Get that ball in play," Coach screamed.

For a moment, Phillip wasn't sure if B.B. was going to throw it. Then she reared back and shot it like a bullet. The ball headed straight for his heart.

It happened so fast, Phillip didn't have time to consider what to do. Instead, he reached out and caught the ball.

Phillip Edward Stanislaw caught the ball.

The ball thrown by B.B. Tyson.

He froze with it in his hands. The force of the ball stung his fingers and made his hands tingle like he was holding his father's hand buzzer. B.B. was already chasing another ball.

"Holy cow, you caught it," said Shawn, who was standing near Phillip.

"He caught it," Shawn yelled to Coach.

Coach blew his whistle.

The world stopped.

B.B. spun and saw Phillip.

Coach forced words from his mouth like an ill-prepared student, answering with an inflection at the end that changed the statement to a question. "You're out?"

B.B. dropped the ball and marched toward the bleachers.

"That was cool!" one of the kids yelled.

"Yeah, good catch, Cool-slaw," said another.

"Cool-slaw, Cool-slaw," the group chanted.

Phillip felt his ears flush.

"That's enough!" Coach roared. But the cheering continued.

Coach blew his whistle hard.

"I said that's enough."

The noise evaporated.

"Go get changed," said Coach. The color was gone from his face.

A member of the Dodgeballers' Club objected, "But we still have ten minutes left of class."

"Beat it," said Coach. The kids didn't need telling twice.

Phillip saw B.B. sitting on the bleachers. Her arms were around her knees and she had buried her face in them. She didn't look up once as the rest of the kids cleared the gym, leaving her and her father alone.

From outside the gym, Phillip could hear Coach's raised voice. Spying through the wire-covered glass, he could see the anger in Coach's animated hand gestures. For the first time since he'd met B.B. Tyson, Phillip felt sorry for her.

A "fearless" snake charmer actually has little to worry about. A well-fed snake is sluggish and not dangerous. The gentle-looking zebra, however, can be an extremely difficult animal.

When Phillip lived with the circus, he knew the difference between a snake and a zebra. But the Hardingtown Middle School was a different jungle. It was hard to tell who wanted to drape around his shoulder and who wanted to kick him in the pants. Phillip had barely gotten out of his gym clothes when he heard an announcement over the loudspeaker telling him to report to the principal's office. He went to his locker to get his sweatshirt.

"The principal is my pal," Phillip reminded himself as he recalled the poster he had seen on the wall outside of Mr. Race's office last month.

"They're waiting for you in the conference room," the principal's secretary said.

An oval table filled most of the room. Two dark suits sat at the table. One of them was the vice-principal, Mr. Race. The other was the principal, Mr. Bellow, a husky, bushy-eyebrowed man with hairy hands wearing a pin-striped suit.

His necktie was embroidered with dodgeballs. Sitting across from the principals was Aunt Veola.

"Come in, Phillip," said Mr. Race.

Phillip took a seat next to Aunt Veola. She wore a strained expression. In front of her was a copy of the complaint Phillip had filed a few weeks ago, along with his "Request for Preliminary Injunction Hearing." When Sam had first explained to Aunt Veola about the lawsuit, she had told Phillip she was proud of him for standing up against a bully. But would she still support his decision now that she was stuck in the ice chamber with Mr. Race and Mr. Bellow chipping away at her?

"We were just discussing your little research project with your aunt," Mr. Race said.

"You've done an enormously serious thing," Mr. Bellow told Phillip as he smoothed down his bushy eyebrows.

"I'm sorry," Phillip said. "But I don't think the school should force us to play dodgeball. It's too dangerous."

"Have you forgotten where you are?" asked Mr. Race. "In Hardingtown, playing dodgeball is a privilege."

"Yes," agreed Mr. Bellow. "Playing dodgeball is an honor."

Phillip wanted to be respectful, but he felt his mouth open and heard his voice coming out. "Getting my glasses broken was not an honor."

"Young man," Mr. Bellow said, "that bad attitude is not amusing." Phillip looked at the vice-principal. He looked at the principal. Mr. Bellow was right—they did not look amused.

"Veola," said Mr. Race, "you have my sympathies, taking in a boy who is constantly stirring up trouble."

Phillip's eyes stung. He squeezed them shut and tried to think of something else, anything else. Mr. Race has a big face. Mr. Race has braces on his face. Mr. Race ate a shoelace. Now disappear from this place, without a trace. He opened his eyes. The vice-principal was still there.

"A boy who refuses to even try to get along," added Mr. Bellow.

"I'm not an unfair man," Mr. Race said. "I realize that children have poor judgment and frequently make mistakes."

"Frequently," agreed Mr. Bellow. "I don't need to remind you of the fiasco Phillip's mother created with her poor judgment."

Mr. Race ran his tongue across his braces.

Aunt Veola looked away and stared at a spot on the wall.

"We're willing to put this whole misunderstanding with Phillip behind us," Mr. Race said.

"Veola," said Mr. Bellow, "if you will see to it that the lawsuit is withdrawn, the school is willing to forgive and forget."

Aunt Veola paused as if she was thinking it over. Mr. Bellow had an extra-large smile, the kind you see on a chimpanzee when he spreads the flaps of his lips to show his teeth. Phillip imagined Mr. Bellow swinging from the conference room light fixture with a bunch of rotted bananas under one of his hairy arms.

The beat of the clock took over the room until, at last, Aunt Veola spoke.

"Has Phillip broken any school rules?" she asked.

"No, I suppose, technically, he hasn't," Mr. Race admitted. "Nonetheless, when you file a lawsuit against your own school, it does violate the spirit of—"

"Has he . . ." asked Aunt Veola, "broken any laws?"

"Of course not," Mr. Bellow bellowed. "But what kind of a kid sues his own school?"

"Phillip, my nephew, does, and as long as he's broken no school rules or law, I believe this is his decision to make."

Mr. Bellow pressed his apelike knuckles against the table and stood up. He leaned toward Aunt Veola. His brow wrinkled and his eyebrows twisted toward his nose. "Things could turn out badly for the boy," he warned.

Aunt Veola propped her own five-foot frame up against the other side of the table and matched him stare for stare. "Are you making a threat?" she demanded.

"I'm making a promise," Mr. Bellow answered. "I promise that unless you drop this ridiculous lawsuit, every man, woman, and child in Hardingtown will hear about it and will know that you and your family are antidodgeball fanatics."

"Veola," said Mr. Race, "you have always been a respected member of this community. Ask yourself if you want to risk it all for a stubborn child."

"Vice-principal Race," Aunt Veola replied, "you can learn a lot from a stubborn child." She left the office so quickly that Phillip had a hard time keeping up. He hadn't seen anyone that angry since Perzi the Talking Parrot had given away the secret of the vanishing bird trick during a performance.

"B.B. Tyson isn't the only bully in Hardingtown Middle School," Aunt Veola muttered as they got into her car.

Phillip wasn't sure what Aunt Veola meant. The whole meeting had been strange. It was like they knew something he didn't.

She flipped open her glove compartment and fished out her driving gloves.

Mr. Bellow had said, "I don't need to remind you of the fiasco Phillip's mother created with her poor judgment."

Fiasco? Phillip had heard that word before. But where?

Then he remembered. It was in the snack bar, when Sam was telling him about the worst fiasco in Hardingtown dodgeball history—the Dodgeball Cheerleader Fiasco.

"The girl," Phillip said as Aunt Veola turned her ignition key, "the base cheerleader. She was my mom, wasn't she?"

The engine made a grinding sound. It died. Aunt Veola suddenly looked like she had, too. "I'm so sorry, Phillip." Her voice was strained. "I should have said something."

"It's okay," said Phillip. "Sam told me about it."

"No, that's not what I mean. I should have said something when Stinky threw the ball."

"You saw him do it?" asked Phillip.

Aunt Veola looked away.

"Of course you did," said Phillip, thinking out loud. "You were the scorekeeper. If anyone had been paying attention, it would have been you."

"I should have told them it was Stinky's fault, not Matilda's. I was afraid if I said anything I would be an outcast. But the guilt from not saying anything was worse. I felt like I was covered in dirt." Phillip wondered if that was why Aunt Veola was always cleaning her hands and wiping things with disinfectant.

"Then Matilda ran away and disappeared," she said. "Most people still think it was her fault, that she was showing off by trying to hold up too many cheerleaders."

Aunt Veola removed a handkerchief from her pocket and wiped her steering wheel. She tried the ignition again and the engine leaped to life. Her voice was so shaky, it made the car seem like it was wobbling, too.

"They say that nobody told on Stinky, but they're wrong. Felix did. He told the principal what he saw. He made the mistake of forgetting to take off his mascot uniform when he did it. You can't blame the principal for not believing him. It's hard for people to take someone seriously when he's dressed like a giant dodgeball with a stuffed hedgehog hanging off."

Phillip silently agreed.

"But Felix tried, God bless him," she continued. "I could never forgive myself for not going with him. But Felix forgave me. He loved me anyway. Forgive and forget, that's his motto. I guess the forgiving is worth the forgetting."

Aunt Veola's face softened, and her driving became smoother.

"I'm glad you told me," Phillip said. He wanted to ask Aunt Veola for more details about the fiasco. Where did his mother go when she disappeared? Whatever happened to Stinky? But he figured maybe he should be quiet and try not to further upset Aunt Veola. He had caused enough of a commotion for one day.

19

When the circus comes to town, local people are often hired to do odd jobs. To ensure they get paid before the circus pulls up stakes, local authorities used to remove a nut from the wagon wheel of the circus office. Consequently, a "nut," in circus lingo, is a term for the daily cost of operating a show. A "nut," in the vocabulary of public school children, is a person who does something that seems insane, like suing your uncle's boss.

Phillip knew that Uncle Felix would be home after dinner. Aunt Veola said it was Phillip's job to tell Uncle Felix about his lawsuit. He should have told him earlier, but talking to Uncle Felix always seemed to make things worse, so he had kept putting it off.

Aunt Veola had been wonderfully understanding about the lawsuit, even supportive. But Uncle Felix might react differently. After all, he worked at the dodgeball factory. How would Uncle Felix feel about his nephew suing his employer?

When they pulled up to the house, Uncle Felix was sitting on the front stoop. A worried expression came across Aunt Veola's face.

"Tell me you came home early because you're sick or something," she said.

"It was something," he answered.

"Fired again?" she asked.

"Now, Veola, it wasn't my fault."

"They don't fire people for nothing," she said. She pushed past him and went into the house.

"It really wasn't my fault," Uncle Felix said to Phillip. "You believe me, right?"

"I do believe you," Phillip said. I should tell him about the lawsuit now, he thought. Whatever the reason they told him he was fired, the real reason was the lawsuit.

As if on cue, Uncle Felix asked, "Do you know why I got fired?"

Phillip nodded.

"It was that missing screw. If it wasn't for that missing screw, the door to the seaming machine would have stayed shut. You can't let dust get into the machinery. Who would be dumb enough to leave the door open?"

"It wasn't the screw," Phillip said. "It was me."

"What are you talking about?"

"I sued the dodgeball factory. I didn't want Aunt Veola to have to pay for my new glasses."

"You did what?" Uncle Felix asked.

"I didn't think about what would happen to you. They fired you because I sued the factory."

For the first time since he had met Uncle Felix, the man was rendered momentarily speechless. Then a sly smile spread across his face.

"I'll be doggoned," Uncle Felix said.

"I apologize for getting you fired," said Phillip.

"You didn't get me fired," Uncle Felix said. He motioned for Phillip to move closer. "It wasn't the screw either. That was something I cooked up for Veola so she wouldn't hit me with a frying pan. The truth is, I forgot—" He looked around nervously and lowered his voice. "I forgot to put the lid on the toilet seat down after I used it."

"They can fire you for that?"

"Actually the company president fired me for using her private bathroom instead of the employees' restroom. Forgetting to put the seat down is how I got caught."

Phillip didn't know what to say.

"That's the third time this year I've lost my job for forgetting to do something." Listening to Uncle Felix talk about his troubles was kind of weird. No grown-up had ever confided in Phillip before. He wanted to help. Uncle Felix was a good guy, just forgetful. He wasn't that different from Phillip's dad. Both were clownish. Except his dad had found a way to turn it into a career. Sam was right—that was kind of cool.

But the important thing right now was to help Uncle Felix find a new job. Phillip went straight to Sam, who agreed that he would ask around. Within a few days, with Sam's help, Uncle Felix had a new job as a cargo loader at the Hardingtown Airport.

Sam also gave Phillip an update on what was happening in the lawsuit. There was grim news.

"I got a call from an old friend who works at the trophy shop," Sam explained as they sat at their usual table. "Seems the lawyers for the dodgeball factory are poking around asking questions about you."

"Why?" asked Phillip.

"They're digging up dirt for the hearing, most likely," said Sam.

"I don't understand."

"These lawyers are out to win, and they may stoop to taking cheap shots if they think it will help."

"How?" Phillip asked.

"It's like this," explained Sam. "If they ask you questions about your parents and circus life, it may fluster you, get you upset, and make you look foolish."

"It won't bother me," said Phillip, nibbling a ketchupy chip. "Everybody already knows I came from the circus."

"Do they know your mother is the fat lady? Do they know you have a morbid fear of custard pie? Do they know your father is a clown, and that he does a gag wearing a baby diaper and bottle?"

Phillip felt his ears flush. "Can't you stop them?"

"I can try," said Sam. "But the bottom line is that you have a decision to make. Are you willing to continue with your lawsuit even if it all comes out?"

Phillip imagined a banner hanging across Hardingtown Middle School that said:

PHILLIP EDWARD COLESLAW IS A PIE-FEARING, ELEPHANT-POOP-SCOOPER WITH A DIAPER-WEARING CLOWN DAD AND A FAT-LADY MOM.

"I made you promise not to quit," Sam said, "but I don't want you to get hurt worse. So I'm releasing you from your promise. If you want to drop the lawsuit rather than have the whole school find out about your family, if you're afraid to go on, I'll understand."

Phillip leaned back in his chair. Its legs made a squeaky sound against the floor. How had things gotten this out of hand? All he wanted was to be a regular kid. Maybe he should drop the lawsuit. Mr. Race said it was wrong for a kid to sue his own school. Maybe he was right.

"What do you think I should do?" Phillip asked Sam.

"It's your decision," Sam said.

Phillip thought about what would happen if he quit. He thought about going back to school and having to play dodgeball again. He thought about watching the kids getting beaned and bumped and slammed and whacked and hearing them being called sissies if they didn't pretend to enjoy it. He thought about Stinky throwing the dodgeball at his mother and of all the people who saw but were too scared to do anything about it. If he did nothing, would he, like Aunt Veola, spend the rest of his life regretting it? Phillip took a deep breath.

"I don't want to drop the lawsuit," he said, "and I'm not afraid to go on."

20

The Windy Van Hooten Circus once put up posters announcing that a genuine unicorn would be performing in their show. One morning, the animal arrived in a large wooden crate. Phillip, expecting a one-horned horse, was disappointed to find a one-horned goat. His mom explained that the word *unicorn* simply means "one horn." So the circus wasn't really lying when it said it had a genuine unicorn.

Phillip wasn't really lying to Sam when he told him he wasn't afraid to continue the lawsuit. At the time, he hadn't been scared. But now it was Monday, he was at school, and B.B. Tyson was coming down the hall.

Phillip slammed his locker shut so he could hurry off, but the sleeve of his shirt got caught in the door. B.B. was headed straight for him. He twisted and pulled to yank the cloth free. But it was too late. He was trapped. Phillip hid his stuck arm behind his back and tried to look casual.

"I need to talk to you," B.B. said. She was so close, he could smell her mint toothpaste. "Somewhere private."

"No," said Phillip, discreetly trying to tug his sleeve free. "Here."

B.B. shot him a funny look. The hallway crowds had thinned and the remaining kids were heading toward their classrooms.

"Okay," she said. "It's about your lawsuit. I want you to know how I feel about it."

Phillip glanced around uncomfortably. She was going to clobber him, then and there. He didn't need the whole school to see it. On the other hand, she wasn't likely to beat him to death in front of witnesses.

"I've never seen my dad so angry," she said, "and Vice-principal Race, too. All because of some nobody kid. It was so . . . so . . ."

B.B. raised her arm, and Phillip readied himself for the blow.

"So cool," she said. "I mean, here I am thinking you're completely spineless because you don't like to play dodge-ball. Then you pick a fight with the whole school, with the whole town."

She flipped a strand of hair out of her eyes and tucked it behind her ear. "There's hope for you yet."

Phillip's mouth was still hanging open as he watched her zip off to class. Suddenly, a hand grabbed his free shoulder.

"Phillip, geez, where you been?" It was Shawn, breathing heavy like he'd been running. "There's something I have to tell you."

"What?" asked Phillip, still half dazed from his encounter with B.B.

"You have to swear not to let anyone know I told you."

"Okay," said Phillip.

"Swear it," demanded Shawn.

"I swear," said Phillip, crossing his heart with his free hand.

"A bunch of kids were talking. Their parents work at the dodgeball factory. Next dodgeball game, they're going to try to put you out of commission."

"How many kids?" Phillip asked.

"More than you can handle," said Shawn. "If you want my advice, the only way you're not going to get hurt in gym class is if you make sure you get hurt *before* gym class. Catch my drift?"

Phillip caught it. He was suggesting Phillip fake an injury to get out of gym class. Phillip decided he would take Shawn's advice. He would bandage a finger. When Coach asked him what had happened, he would say he had slammed his locker door on himself. It wouldn't be a complete lie.

"Thanks," he said.

He watched as Shawn and the other kids scurried off to class, leaving him all by himself. Strangely, for the first time since he arrived in Hardingtown, he didn't feel alone. Shawn was on his side. Even more amazing, B.B. Tyson had chosen not to beat him to death. Phillip felt like things might finally be starting to go his way. Until he remembered his sleeve was still stuck in the locker.

21

After an hour and a half of hanging upside down, even the best acrobat will get dizzy and take a break. Just thinking about all the dodgeballs that had whizzed his way since his first dodgeball game made Phillip dizzy. Hadn't he earned a break, too?

Coach scarcely cared when Phillip showed his bandaged finger and asked to sit out. Phillip had feared he would have to go to the nurse's office and get a note. Instead, Coach treated him like an insect not worth swatting.

Phillip climbed to the top of the bleachers like he was ascending a throne. He would be immune to the chaos below. But as soon as he was there and felt the cold, hard wood beneath him, he wondered if he had done the right thing.

The kids picked teams and went to their respective sides. A couple of them glanced up at Phillip. He hoped they understood. Once he'd won the injunction, they'd be safe, too. Until then, he had to save himself, especially with a whole gang after him.

Coach put the first ball on the line, then the second, and the third. With each ball, Phillip felt his heart beating harder, like the quickening pace of a drum. Coach looked up at Phillip. It felt as if he knew Phillip's thoughts.

"B.B.," Coach yelled, "grab another ball." The gym was so silent you could hear the sound of her sneakers squeaking across the floor. Coach took the ball and added it to the line.

"Let the game begin," he said. He blew his whistle.

A girl with asthma was the first to go down, felled by a boy with straight aim and a crooked nose. Others started getting picked off. With four balls in play, some of the kids were getting hit by more than one ball at once. The smell of dirty socks was quickly overpowered by the stench of drenched underarms.

B.B. and a tall, skinny kid, both armed with balls, squared off in a showdown. Phillip recognized the kid. His mom worked at the dodgeball factory. Why was he going after B.B.?

"Hey, rat," the big kid said. "Here's a piece of cheese for you." He flung the dodgeball like a grenade. B.B. deflected it with the ball in her hands. Then she slammed her ball straight at the kid, tripping his right leg.

"You're out," Coach yelled.

Two more kids whose parents worked at the factory raced over to get a piece of B.B. She dodged the first ball with ease. The second nearly got her.

"Bring it on!" she shouted to the other team. And they did. One against one. Two against one. Three against one. Each time, she dodged their rounds and returned their fire. It only provided them more ammunition. Finally, it was four against one.

They stood barely behind their line: a twelve-year-old with a chip on his shoulder and a long scar across his chin;

his human-tank friend; a girl with thick arm muscles and stringy hair; and the boy with the crooked nose. They teasingly tossed their balls in the air, knowing they had her. Not even B.B. Tyson could handle a four-ball assault. She was tired, weakened. She needed to rest. B.B. turned to retreat but bumped into a kid hiding behind her. They crashed to the ground. The kid crawled backward in a crab walk. B.B. turned and looked across the line, chin up, chest out, waiting to feel the first strike.

"Wait!" Phillip yelled. He couldn't bear to see B.B. get pummeled. He had to do something.

"Stop the game!" He raced down the bleachers and over to Coach. A shrill whistle froze the dodgeballers in place and gave B.B. a temporary reprieve.

"What do you think you're doing?" Coach asked.

Phillip ripped the bandage from his finger. "It's not hurt," he said. "It was a lie."

"You're the strangest kid I've ever met," said Coach.

"Am I in the game?" Phillip asked.

"You're in," he said.

B.B. was still draped like a rug on the floor, with the four gorillas ready to beat her. Phillip raced over.

"Are you okay?" he asked. She nodded, but the look in her eyes said they were still in trouble. She got up and stood next to Phillip.

Coach's whistle revived the action.

"Isn't that cute," the girl with thick arm muscles teased. "B.B.'s got a boyfriend. Bye-bye, boyfriend."

She pitched the ball hard at Phillip's head. He jumped up and caught it. Immediately, the crooked-nosed boy lobbed another ball at him. It headed straight for Phillip's stomach.

He threw the first ball up in the air and caught the second ball. When the first ball began to come back down, he instinctively started juggling the two balls. He kept them high in the air like he had been taught. A trickle of sweat ran down Phillip's forehead as he concentrated.

"Look out," screamed B.B. as she dove in front of him and caught the third ball, fired by the human tank.

"Thanks," said Phillip, still juggling. "Toss it here." She tossed the third ball at him, and it was swallowed into the juggling mass.

Chip-and-scar boy held the fourth ball. He slammed it toward B.B.'s torso while she was watching Phillip. She turned to grab it as it was about to pelt her in the stomach. The force of the ball knocked her back, and she stumbled before getting her footing. She hoisted the fourth ball triumphantly in the air. Her teammates began cheering wildly.

Wrrrrrrrrrrrr! Coach's whistle pierced the air.

"That's enough of that juggling nonsense," he said. "Get those balls back into play."

"There's no rule against juggling," said Shawn.

"That's right," another kid agreed. "You go, Cool-slaw."

Coach blew his whistle, but Phillip did not stop. Coach's face began to turn grayish-blue. Still, the whistle could not be heard above the cheers.

After Phillip got more height on the dodgeballs, he motioned for B.B. to toss in the last one. She glanced at her father's angry face, then back at Phillip. She tossed the ball to Phillip and grinned. He didn't stop juggling until the bell rang.

During his walk to the courthouse after school, Phillip kept replaying the scene in his mind. He had died and gone to dodgeball heaven. That was the only explanation for what had occurred. When he got to the courthouse, Aunt Veola told him that his new glasses were ready and that they would be picking them up that night. Phillip went straight to the snack bar to tell Sam all that had happened.

"B.B.'s really changed. I don't think she's going to bully me again, and I don't want to sue her anymore. Suing the dodgeball factory and the school is enough. I want to drop B.B. from the lawsuit."

Sam didn't agree.

"It's not that simple," he said.

"Why not?" Phillip asked. "Why can't I drop B.B. from the lawsuit?"

"If you drop the assault charge against B.B. now, another bully will figure he can hit another kid and not have to worry. If you let one bully get away with something, you're letting all bullies get away with it."

Phillip could see his mother inside the gymnasium on the day of the Regional High School Championship game, her hedgehog-colored cheerleading ribbons drooping in limp ponytails. He pictured her trying to block out the shouts and jeers of the accusing crowd, and then fleeing in defeat.

Sam was right. The lawsuit wasn't only about him and B.B. It was about kids everywhere standing up for themselves. He had to keep going, even against B.B.

"I understand," said Phillip.

"I'm glad," said Sam. "Because our hearing is set for Monday morning."

Phillip dropped his root beer. The foaming brew splashed across the table and dripped onto the floor. Because they had asked the court for an injunction, the judge wanted to hear the case right away. Sam explained a bunch of other legal stuff, too. As Phillip grabbed napkins and mopped up the mess, all he could think was that the hearing would be here in no time.

If he lost the case in court, the dodgeball bullies would be waiting for him and his friends. All his hard work would have been for nothing. The kids on the bleachers, Sam, Aunt Veola, Uncle Felix—even, somehow, his mom—he would let them all down. He would be a loser—the official laughing-stock of the Unofficial Dodgeball Capital of the World.

22

Pink lemonade was created accidentally by a circus vendor who used a bucket of water that another performer had washed her red tights in. Whenever someone is being careless because they're rushing, circus performers say they're "making pink lemonade."

The morning of his hearing Phillip did not want to make pink lemonade. He took his time getting ready, loading his briefcase with legal books and papers. It was really a suitcase from the attic that looked like a briefcase but was bigger. Phillip couldn't understand why lawyers paid extra to buy smaller bags.

He wore black pants and a white button-down shirt. A too-long necktie, which he had borrowed from Uncle Felix, was knotted clumsily around his thin neck. Since he didn't own any dress shoes, he wore sneakers.

Phillip took so long getting ready, Aunt Veola left without him, and Uncle Felix had to drive him to the courthouse. Uncle Felix's lime green Volkswagen beetle made a *putt-putt* sound as they chugged down the street. After the car passed the dodgeball factory, it began to sputter. In less than a block, the engine stalled.

"There must be a leak in my gas tank," Uncle Felix said. "Don't worry, there's a gas station ahead, and it's downhill from here."

Oh no, thought Phillip. I can't be late.

Uncle Felix put the car in neutral. Phillip got out and pushed. He had to lean his shoulder into it to get the car rolling while Uncle Felix steered it into Friendly's Gas-'n-Go. A sign advertised the Special of the Month for November was a free dodgeball poster with each oil change.

An old man and woman in matching dirty blue overalls shuffled over. Phillip had seen them before snuggling together on the bench outside of the shop, waiting for customers. The woman washed the windshield. The old man reached for the gas nozzle.

"Hey, Felix," the old man said. "Coasting again, huh?" He flipped a switch and the meter on the pump began to run. The gas

fumes made Phillip's nose tingle like he was going to sneeze. He hopped back into the passenger seat.

"You want I should fill out a credit-card slip?" asked the old man. "Or you paying cash?"

Uncle Felix squeezed forward and reached for his back pocket. "I must have left my wallet in my other pants."

"Again?" the old man asked.

Phillip reached into the glove box and grabbed a white handkerchief. He unfolded it and gave Uncle Felix a crisp twenty-dollar bill.

"Where did this come from?" Uncle Felix asked.

"Aunt Veola hid it there just in case, because you're always forgetting to put gas in the car," Phillip said. "Now, can we hurry? I've got to get to court."

"Don't forget," yelled the old man as they putt-putted away, "next month we give out a free ticket for the Annual Dodgeball World Series and Barbecue with every tune-up."

Uncle Felix was already late for his new job at the airport, so he dropped off Phillip at the front steps of the courthouse. Phillip was strangely relieved they had run out of gas. After that, what else could go wrong?

Inside the courthouse, he got in line for the metal detector. This time, it felt different.

"Good morning, Phillip," Aunt Veola said.

"Hello, Aunt Veola," Phillip replied. He placed his lucky marble and a paper-clip chain into the plastic change box.

"You'll have to go through this time," she said, "since you'll be going into a courtroom."

Phillip dropped his briefcase onto the conveyor belt and walked through the metal detector. It did not make a sound.

"You're supposed to meet Sam in courtroom number two," she told him. "I'll be up to watch when this rush is over."

Past the security area, Phillip noticed that the courthouse lobby looked especially crowded.

"Excuse me, pardon me," he said, trying to get through.

"Hey, Phillip, over here," he heard a familiar voice yell. It was Shawn O'Malley. "Wait up," Shawn said. There was a man with him. The man wore a tweed sports jacket and held an electronic device. Close up, Phillip could see it was a tape recorder.

"Phillip," Shawn said, a little out of breath. "This is my grandfather's dentist's brother. He's a reporter for the *Hardingtown Star Tribune*. I told him you'd give him an interview."

"What?" asked Phillip. "Why would you want to interview me?"

"Don't be modest. You and your lawsuit are big news today," the reporter said. He flipped the switch to his tape recorder. "Let's start with background questions." He pushed the microphone in front of Phillip's face. "Is it true that you were born in a circus tent?"

"Excuse me," Phillip said. He grabbed Shawn by the arm and tugged him away so they could talk privately.

"What are you doing here?" Phillip asked Shawn.

"Everybody's here," Shawn said. "Practically the whole sixth grade. When Mr. Race heard your case was going to trial, he declared it a school field trip. Said it would teach us kids a lesson. He thinks you're gonna lose. But me and some of the other kids, we think you got a chance."

"Are you Phillip Stanislaw?" an attractive Hispanic woman asked. "He's over here," she shouted to a man with a television camera on his shoulder.

"Oh no, you don't," said the newspaper reporter. "I saw him first."

While the television reporter and the newspaper reporter argued, Phillip fled to the old part of the courthouse and the freight elevator. He took the elevator to the second floor and didn't stop moving until he was in courtroom number two.

It was even more crowded inside the courtroom than the lobby. A vast assortment of people filled the spectator seating, packed together like a circus audience on Free Peanut Night. The last rows of seats were filled with sixth-graders, craning their necks to get a better view.

There was a wooden railing that separated the courtroom proper, behind which were a table and chairs on the left and another set on the right. At the left table, Phillip saw a pair of men and a woman in dark suits. At the right table, he saw Sam and an empty chair, which he quickly filled. Sam pointed out the defendants' lawyers: Mr. Dinkle, the boss attorney, and his assistants, Ms. Jones and Mr. Terry.

Sam also told Phillip that because of the special relief they had sought, a judge instead of a jury would be deciding the case.

"The good news," said Sam, "is that the judge who's been assigned to our case isn't a dodgeball fan."

"That is good news," agreed Phillip.

"The bad news is that she coaches a recreational soccer team for senior citizens called 'Golden Toes.'"

"Why is that bad news?" asked Phillip.

"It may make her identify more with the defendants and make her lean their way."

"Will she try to be fair?" asked Phillip.

"I hope so," said Sam.

Phillip noticed a pitcher of water on his table and poured them both a tall glass. He also noticed a small trash can next to the table and moved it closer, just in case he had to throw up.

"Hear ye, hear ye," said the court tipstaff, the judge's courtroom helper. "All rise for the Honorable Ida E. Monn."

Boffo, the three-legged circus poodle, lost his leg in a bicycle accident, and they said he would never ride again. The leg was buried behind the ticket tent. Each day, Boffo would dig holes around the tent trying to find his leg. Each evening, the circus moved to another town. Boffo never did find his leg, but his other legs became so strong from all that digging that he was able to start riding again. Whenever a situation seemed hopeless, Phillip's mom would remind him about Boffo.

Phillip was thinking about Boffo as Judge Monn entered the courtroom in a swirl of black robe. A judge is like a referee, Sam had explained. Her job is to make sure people play by the rules and don't misbehave.

Phillip thought Judge Monn's black robe made her look more like the grim reaper than a referee. She had silver hair and a neutral expression. The judge surveyed her courtroom like it was a soccer field and tossed herself into her chair. Everyone sat.

"Let's get this hearing started," said Judge Monn. "Are there any matters to be dealt with before we begin?"

Mr. Dinkle rushed to a podium. Although his hair was also

gray, his step seemed quite lively. Phillip wondered if Mr. Dinkle colored his hair to make himself look older.

"Good morning, Your Honor," Mr. Dinkle said. "The defense would like to present this Motion to Disqualify Opposing Counsel." Phillip looked to Sam for a translation.

"They want the judge to tell me I can't be your lawyer," Sam whispered to Phillip.

"Can they do that?" Phillip asked. But Sam had already stood up. He buttoned the jacket of his tailor-made suit.

"Stop dragging your feet," Judge Monn said to Mr. Dinkle, "and tell me why."

"Conflict of interest," said Mr. Dinkle. "Yesterday, we hired Mr. Phoenix's son to work for our law firm. A lawyer shouldn't try a case when a close relative works for the law firm on the other side."

"Of all the low-down tricks," said Sam. "The only reason you hired him was so you could try to get me disqualified."

Sam and Mr. Dinkle began arguing. Phillip wished they would stick to the facts about how B.B. Tyson broke his glasses. What would he do if the judge wouldn't let Sam try the case? Phillip remembered something he had read in a law book. He needed to get Sam's attention, but there were no salt and pepper shakers for their secret signal. Phillip picked up the the drinking glasses.

"If Mr. Stanislaw cannot find replacement counsel," said Mr. Dinkle, "he'll have to withdraw his lawsuit."

Phillip banged the glasses together.

Cling! Cling! Cling! Cling!

"What is that annoying sound?" asked Judge Monn.

"I believe," said Sam, "my client is signaling that he wishes to speak."

Phillip stood up and cleared his voice so that his words wouldn't sound too squeaky.

"Yes, ma'am," he said. "I would like to know if it would solve the problem if I had another lawyer."

"Well, of course," said Judge Monn. "That's the whole reason I've been hearing arguments. Do you have another lawyer?"

"Yes, ma'am," said Phillip. The courtroom was so quiet you could hear a feather drop. Phillip's knees wobbled. He wasn't sure that he could force out the words.

"Don't let the grass grow under your feet," said Judge Monn. "Out with it. Who is this lawyer?"

"Me, ma'am," Phillip said, trying to sound certain. "I would like to represent myself."

A hum like the static from a broken speaker crept through the room. Judge Monn beat her gavel against her mahogany desk.

"Objection!" the three dodgeball defense lawyers screamed in unison as they sprang from their seats.

"He can't practice law without a license," Mr. Dinkle said.

"You only need a license when you represent another person," said Sam. "The Constitution of the United States ensures the right of a party to a lawsuit to represent himself."

The lawyers began bickering again. Phillip hit the glasses together until they stopped. Judge Monn uncovered her ears and ordered the tipstaff to remove the glasses from Phillip's table.

"Young man," Judge Monn said to Phillip. "If you wish to address this court you will do so like the other attorneys. You will rise from your seat, say the word *objection,* and wait for this court to recognize you."

Phillip didn't understand why the law had so many strange rules. When he was in the law library, he had found a whole book about odd laws. The laws made it illegal to carry an ice-cream cone in your pocket in parts of Kentucky, to sleep on a refrigerator in Pittsburgh, and to walk across the street on your hands in Connecticut. Still, he wasn't about to argue with the judge.

"Yes, Your Honor," said Phillip. He stood up and adjusted his pants down a little at the waist so he wouldn't get a wedgie.

"It seems to me," Phillip said, "that if the Constitution says I can represent myself, and Mr. Dinkle says I can't, then the Constitution should win."

"This is ridiculous," Mr. Dinkle said. "Your Honor, the boy is only eleven years old."

"That's true," Phillip said. "But do you have a legal case that says that an eleven-year-old can't be his own lawyer?" The judge looked over at Mr. Dinkle.

"He's got you there, doesn't he?" said Sam. Mr. Dinkle folded his arms against his chest in a dramatic display of exasperation.

Judge Monn leaned back in her chair and rocked. "You consider yourself a bit of a rabble-rouser, don't you, son?" she asked Phillip.

"No," he answered. "I just like to read."

"You don't know what kind of trouble you're asking for when you say you want to represent yourself," said Judge Monn, "do you?"

"Probably not," Phillip admitted.

"I ought to let you go ahead in order to teach you a lesson," she said.

"Thank you," said Phillip. "Please let me know if I'm making any mistakes."

"I'm sure Mr. Dinkle will keep you informed on that front."

"Yes, indeed," said Mr. Dinkle. "In fact, after further consideration, the defendants wish to withdraw their objection. If Mr. Stanislaw wishes to represent himself, we would be delighted." The three lawyers began to snicker.

"The objection having been withdrawn," ruled Judge Monn, "this court will permit Mr. Stanislaw to represent himself."

When the gavel hit, a news photographer stood up and a flash went off in Phillip's direction. Muffled clapping snuck from the last row of spectator seating. Phillip looked back and saw Shawn and his cousin smile.

Phillip felt like smiling, too, until he heard Judge Monn say, "You may call your first witness, Mr. Stanislaw."

24

Bruno's Nightmare is a complicated three-person juggling pattern sometimes used in circus acts. Phillip's nightmare was suddenly realizing he was in charge of his lawsuit and had no idea what to do next.

"Now what?" Phillip whispered to his friend. Sam ruffled through a box of file folders with Braille-coded edges. He handed Phillip a thick document titled "Plaintiff's Trial Memorandum."

"Find the page that says witness list," Sam instructed him. Phillip found it and read the first name.

"My first witness is Marvin Nerp," he announced to the judge. A puny man in a brown polyester business suit rose from the defendants' table and swaggered over to the stand. He had a pencil-thin mustache and oily-smelling hair brushed back to cover a balding spot on the back of his head. While the tipstaff was swearing in the witness, Phillip asked Sam, "Who is this guy?"

"He owns the dodgeball factory," Sam said. "Get him to admit that the dodgeballs his company makes are supposed to be used to hit children."

Phillip noticed that the room had gone quiet.

"We're waiting, Mr. Stanislaw," Judge Monn said.

He forced himself to his feet, opened his mouth, and tried to sound like a real lawyer.

"Good morning, Mr. Nerd," Phillip said.

"Nerp," the witness corrected him. "My name is Marvin Nerp."

"Did you say Twerp?" Judge Monn asked.

"No," the witness thundered, "Nerp! I said Nerp!"

Giggles escaped from the back of the courtroom. Mr. Dinkle delivered a cold, hard stare to the rows of school-children that advised them it had better not happen again.

"Mr. Nerp," said Phillip, "do you make dodgeballs?"

"My company makes dodgeballs," he said. "I am Chief Executive Officer of the American Dodgeball Company."

"What are dodgeballs for?" asked Phillip.

"What are they for?" Mr. Nerp repeated. "What a stupid question. They're for playing dodgeball, of course."

"Okay," said Phillip. "I guess you can leave." The witness looked strangely at Phillip then over at his own lawyer, Mr. Dinkle, who was already on his feet.

"Your Honor, I would like to ask a few questions of the witness on cross-examination," said Mr. Dinkle. "If Mr. Stanislaw doesn't mind."

"No," said Phillip. "I don't mind."

"Mr. Nerp," said Mr. Dinkle, "thank you for taking time out of your busy schedule. I know you are an important man, and you are needed back at the factory where you employ one-fifth of the workforce of this humble city. So I will be brief."

It took Mr. Dinkle nearly an hour to be brief. He asked Mr. Nerp questions about the dodgeball factory. He also asked him about charity work. Mr. Nerp testified about how he didn't lay people off during years when his profits were low. He even testified about how something called the capital-gains tax was the work of the Devil.

Phillip could not imagine what these things had to do with his lawsuit, but he was grateful that Mr. Dinkle had chosen to be brief, and he wondered how long the question-ing would have gone on had he not. When Mr. Dinkle was finally done, the judge asked Phillip if he had any more ques-tions for the witness.

"Only one," said Phillip. "Mr. Nerp, are children supposed to use your dodgeballs to hit other children?"

"Yes," answered Mr. Nerp.

"Okay," said Phillip. He sat down.

Scattered clapping drifted from the last row of spectator seating.

"Call your next witness," the judge ordered Phillip, sound-ing like a circus announcer preparing the audience for the next act of the show. Phillip picked up the witness list and read the next name.

"I call Francis Lee Tyson," said Phillip.

He looked out into the crowd to see who it would be. A chair at the defendants' table slid backward and Coach Tyson stood up.

Phillip almost wet his pants.

"Your Honor," he asked excitedly, "please, may I go to the bathroom?"

"You've already called the witness," the judge said. "Can't you wait?"

"I've really got to go," said Phillip.

Judge Monn sighed. "The court will be in recess for five

minutes." She banged her gavel and everyone stood. "Please remain in the courtroom, except, of course, for you, Mr. Stanislaw." The second Judge Monn disappeared into her judicial chambers, the courtroom erupted with the sound of gossiping spectators.

Phillip felt hundreds of eyes on him as he made his way to the door. A group of kids whose parents worked at the dodgeball factory glared at him menacingly. Mr. Race was sitting in the back row closest to the door. He sneered at Phillip, his braces shining like jagged shark teeth. Phillip yanked the door open so hard he nearly knocked himself over. He stood with his back against it on the other side, trying to remember if he needed to breathe in or out.

Last time he had wanted to talk to Coach—at school when B.B. got out of his car—Phillip didn't have the nerve to face him. How could he question Coach now in front of a whole roomful of people?

25

Using arrows to mark the way is a circus tradition. Before the Windy Van Hooten Circus moves from one town to the next, the twenty-four-hour advance man marks the route with a system of red arrows. It's the only way to make sure the dancing bears don't end up in Pittsburgh and the dancing bears' food in Cleveland.

As Phillip looked for the closest bathroom, he wished the upstairs hallway of the Hardingtown County Courthouse were marked with arrows. He finally found the men's room next to the main elevator, the elevator that could take him down to the ground floor, where he could sneak out the back of the building and run away from the whole thing. Phillip looked at the men's-room door. He looked at the elevator door.

Inside the courtroom, the buzz died down, and the spectators, grateful for the five-minute stretch, took their seats. Judge Monn reentered.

"All rise," the tipstaff said. The judge settled herself and looked over at Phillip's empty chair.

"Where is Mr. Stanislaw?" she asked. The courtroom door squeaked open and Phillip peeked in.

"Sorry, ma'am," Phillip said, "I'm stuck." Holding one hand on his pants zipper and the other on his waist, he reluctantly entered the room. The teeth of his pants zipper were held fast to a piece of necktie that jutted out from the crotch of his pants. The courtroom shook with laughter.

"Tipstaff," Judge Monn said, "will you please assist Mr. Stanislaw with his . . . predicament." He took Phillip into the hallway to help him jiggle the necktie free from the zipper.

"Don't worry," said the tipstaff, "it happens all the time." Phillip could hear snickers from the courtroom.

"They're laughing at me," he said.

"Ignore it," said the tipstaff. "Those high-price lawyers are trying to get to you."

"It's not so much the lawyers," said Phillip. "I just wish my classmates weren't here. It makes it so much harder."

"That's why Stinky brought them."

"Stinky?"

"Stinky Race. Your vice-principal. That's what we used to call him when we were in school."

Suddenly, it all made sense.

"He's the bully who threw the dodgeball at my mom when she was holding up the cheerleader pyramid," said Phillip. "It was Mr. Race, wasn't it?"

"I didn't see it happen," said the tipstaff. "I had my back turned." He pulled at the zipper, but it wouldn't budge. "Old Stinky sure got his reward for that dirty trick."

"What do you mean?" asked Phillip.

"Guess who landed on *him*?"

Phillip pictured his mom, younger but not lighter, as she struggled to keep her balance so the pyramid wouldn't fall. She soared forward, then back. Her trusting friends above her were helplessly yanked like kites in the wind. Finally, she lurched forward, stopping mere feet from Stinky—when her knees buckled. Phillip could hear Stinky scream as he was swallowed in the giant folds of her cheerleading uniform.

"It took a team of dentists seven hours to wire Stinky's teeth back together," said the tipstaff. "They've never been able to get them completely straight." He gave a final yank, and the cloth broke free from the zipper.

"There you go, kid."

"Thank you." Phillip flipped the long part of the necktie over his shoulder and carefully glided up the zipper.

"Stinky is hoping that with your classmates here, you won't have the guts to finish what you started."

"I promised Sam I wouldn't quit," said Phillip. "I promised myself."

The tipstaff straightened Phillip's tie. "Then I guess you better get back in there," he said.

When Phillip reentered the courtroom, Mr. Race gave him another sneer. This time, Phillip sneered back.

Coach was already on the witness stand. The tipstaff swore him in.

"Try to get Coach to admit that he teaches the kids to hit other kids with dodgeballs," Sam advised.

Phillip stared at the carpet in front of the witness stand.

"Coach," he began, then lost his train of thought.

He knew he had to look brave even if he didn't feel it. Whenever the Pork Downs Racing Circus Pigs were performing, you could tell the frightened pigs from the confident ones by looking at their tails. The more relaxed a pig was, the curlier his tail. The straight-tailed pig was never first to the delicious slop at the finish line. Phillip tried to relax his tail.

"Mr. Stanislaw, we're waiting for your question," said Judge Monn. Phillip forced himself to look at Coach. He seemed different without his whistle and cap. Still scary but a little less so.

"Coach Tyson," he said, "do we play dodgeball in gym?"

"You know we do."

"Why?"

"Because this is Hardingtown."

"Do you tell kids they should use the dodgeballs to hit other kids?"

"Of course. That's how you play dodgeball."

"Can't we play something else?"

"Not in Hardingtown. Here we play dodgeball."

Phillip didn't know what else to ask, so he sat down.

Mr. Dinkle asked Coach questions about physical education. Coach talked about how you have to be tough to survive in this world and how playing dodgeball helps toughen kids up. He used terms like "gross motor skills" and "quick reaction times" and "aerobic workout." He did not mention that the kids sometimes called it "slaughter ball" or "killer ball" or "prison ball."

"Did you ever instruct anyone to throw a dodgeball at Mr. Stanislaw?" asked Mr. Dinkle.

"Not specifically," Coach answered.

"Did you ever instruct a student to throw a dodgeball in the face of another student?"

"No."

"Do you have an opinion as to whether or not Ms. Tyson intentionally hit Mr. Stanislaw in the face with the dodgeball?"

"In my opinion," said Coach, "it was an accident."

"Could Mr. Stanislaw have avoided the accident?" Mr. Dinkle asked.

"Yes," said Coach. "He could have moved out of the way."

Phillip felt like a big fat dodgeball had hit him in the stomach. Was it his fault? Should he have jumped out of the way instead of standing his ground? No, he thought, I can't start doubting myself.

"Mr. Stanislaw," said Judge Monn. "Do you have any further questions for this witness?"

Coach scowled.

Phillip shook his head.

"Call your next witness," Judge Monn said.

"My next witness is B.B. Tyson."

B.B. wore a blue dress with tiny, pink flowers and a locket on a gold chain. As she went to the witness stand, she suddenly seemed to walk like a girl. The tipstaff had B.B. put one hand on a Bible and the other hand up in the air. Like the other witnesses, she swore to tell the truth, the whole truth, and nothing but the truth.

Phillip had never before been in a place where only the truth could be spoken. He liked it. He didn't have to consult with Sam about questions for B.B. He knew what he wanted to ask.

"Why did you hit me in the head with a dodgeball?"

"Objection!" said Mr. Dinkle. "Lack of foundation and assuming facts not in evidence."

"Sustained," said the judge. To Phillip, they might as well have been speaking pig Latin.

"Mr. Stanislaw," said Judge Monn, "you'll have to begin by establishing who the witness is."

"I already know who she is," said Phillip.

"You have to establish who the witness is for the benefit of the court," said the Judge. "Let's stop pussyfooting around. Just ask her who she is."

Phillip looked at B.B. She was playing with a string hanging from the lace on the sleeve of her dress.

"B.B.," he said, "who are you?"

"State your name for the record," Judge Monn added to speed things along.

"My real name?" she asked. "Like on my birth certificate?"

"Yes," said the judge, "your legal name."

"My name is Barbara Beth Tyson. But nobody calls me that except my grandma."

"Thank you, Ms. Tyson," said the judge. Turning to Phillip, she added, "Now you may continue, Mr. Stanislaw."

"B.B.," said Phillip, "have you ever hit anyone with a dodgeball?"

"Sure," she said, "lots of times."

"Why do you keep doing it?" he asked.

"Because it's gym class, and it's dodgeball, and I'm supposed to hit kids."

"Did you break my glasses?"

"They must have broken when I hit you with the dodgeball," she admitted.

"Okay. Thanks," he said. Phillip sat down. Sam smiled and patted him on the back.

"I have a few questions on cross-examination," Mr. Dinkle said. "Good morning, Barbara. That's a lovely dress."

"My grandma made me wear it."

"How old are you, Barbara?" he asked.

After some hesitation, she answered, "I'm almost thirteen."

"The reason you're still in sixth grade is because you got held back, isn't that true?"

"Yes."

"Why did you get held back?" he asked.

B.B. played with her dress lace. "It was a car accident," she said. "When I was seven years old, I busted my back and had to wear a brace, and I couldn't go to school for a long time."

"Is that the same accident that killed your mother?"

"Yes," said B.B.

"Barbara," Mr. Dinkle said, "when you threw the ball that allegedly broke Mr. Stanislaw's glasses, you didn't mean to, did you?"

"I didn't mean to break his glasses."

"You didn't mean to hurt him, right?"

B.B. was silent. "Do you want to know the truth?" she asked Judge Monn.

"That's why we're here," Judge Monn answered.

"I was mad at him. In the cafeteria, he got meat loaf and peas on me. All the kids saw it. They were expecting me to pay him back."

"Objection," said Mr. Dinkle. "Your Honor, the witness is going far beyond my question."

"Oh, be quiet and sit down," said Judge Monn. "Continue, Ms. Tyson."

"I didn't mean to hit him in the face. When his glasses broke, I was sorry."

"Why didn't you apologize?" asked the judge.

"I wanted to, but I was afraid my dad would think I was wussy. He hates wusses."

Phillip stood up.

"Do you have an objection?" the judge asked Phillip.

"No," Phillip said. "I just wanted to tell B.B. that I think she's brave for telling the truth." B.B. flipped a piece of hair out of her eyes and beamed.

"One more thing," she said, looking at Phillip. "In the cafeteria, it was my leg you tripped over."

"Objection," Mr. Dinkle yelled. "Nobody even asked her a question."

"Sustained. If there are no more questions for this witness," the judge said, "she may step down. Name your next witness, Mr. Stanislaw."

"Your Honor," Phillip said, "I call me to the stand."

26

In the circus world, 'suicide' is a flying-trapeze trick where the performer falls face-first toward the net and doesn't turn until right before hitting it. In the legal world, 'suicide' is a term for what happens when a client decides to represent himself in court.

When he was seated on the witness stand, Phillip said, "Should I ask myself a question?"

"That won't be necessary," said Judge Monn. "Simply explain what you want the court to hear."

"Well," Phillip began, "it happened in gym class. B.B. hit me with the dodgeball and my glasses fell off and broke. It cost two hundred and forty-nine dollars to get new ones. The book I read said that the person who hit you should have to pay for the damages."

"Is that it?" asked the judge.

"I guess."

"Mr. Dinkle, you may cross-examine," said the judge.

The lawyer eyed Phillip like a hawk watching a mouse dart across a field. "You're not from around here, are you, Mr. Stanislaw?"

"I live with my Aunt Veola and Uncle Felix on Bowman's Hill."

"But you haven't always lived there, have you?" Phillip knew what was coming. He was going to have to admit in front of the entire sixth grade that he was raised by a clown and a fat lady.

"Objection," Sam cried, jumping to his feet.

"You can't object," Mr. Dinkle reminded him. "You aren't his lawyer anymore."

"I'm afraid he's right," said Judge Monn. "You'll have to sit down."

Phillip spoke hesitantly, "I've lived with my aunt and uncle since September."

"With whom did you live before that?" asked Mr. Dinkle, smugly.

"My parents."

"And what do your parents do for a living?"

"Objection," yelled Aunt Veola from the back of the courtroom.

"Now, Veola," said Judge Monn, "you've got no more right than Sam to be objecting."

"Well, somebody's got to say something," Aunt Veola said. "You can lose a lot of hens letting a fox run wild in a henhouse."

"I believe I've been insulted," said Mr. Dinkle.

"Why can't you leave the boy's family out of this?" she asked Mr. Dinkle.

"He's the one that chose to bring the lawsuit," said Mr. Dinkle.

"Maybe so," said Aunt Veola, "but only because he had to."

Judge Monn slapped her gavel until they stopped. "Put a sock in it or I'll give you both the boot," she said.

"I can't just sit here and say nothing," said Aunt Veola.

"You can and you will," warned the judge. "Or you will be escorted from this courtroom." A woman sitting next to Aunt Veola tugged on her sleeve, and Aunt Veola reluctantly settled back into her seat.

"Let's get back to business," said the judge.

"Of course, Your Honor," said Mr. Dinkle. "I believe the witness was about to explain what his parents do for a living."

Phillip felt a wave of warmth rising to his ears and spreading across his cheeks. He gazed at the sea of schoolmates. They stared back with expectant faces. How could he tell them about his parents? Mr. Dinkle was wiggling with delight, anticipating the wave of laughter that was about to shake the courtroom.

"I don't understand the question," Phillip said. Brief disappointment swept across Mr. Dinkle.

"How are your parents employed?"

Phillip shrugged. Mr. Dinkle's mouth twisted into a frustrated grimace. Judge Monn turned to Phillip and addressed him directly.

"What don't you understand?" she asked.

"I don't understand," said Phillip, "why Mr. Dinkle is asking me questions about my parents' jobs when it doesn't have anything to do with this lawsuit. Isn't that called 'irrelevant'?"

"You're right," said Judge Monn. "Objection sustained."

Mr. Dinkle whispered something to his assistants, who got up and left the courtroom.

"Wouldn't you admit that the game of dodgeball has its good points?" he asked.

"I can't think of any," Phillip answered. Mr. Dinkle glanced back at the door and then continued.

"Isn't it true that the game provides an excellent, whole-body workout and helps build muscle tone?"

"I don't know," said Phillip. "I've never been in the game long enough to build anything."

The door opened, and Ms. Jones, one of Mr. Dinkle's assistants, slipped in. She gave Mr. Dinkle a thumbs-up signal. He gave her a nod.

"I'd like to show you something that has been marked as Defendants' Exhibit A," said Mr. Dinkle.

He gave Ms. Jones another nod. She threw open the door. Two burly men in work uniforms wheeled in a large, flat dolly. A big cardboard box, nearly three feet wide and four feet high, was on the dolly. It was marked in large black letters with the words DEFENDANTS' EXHIBIT A. The men wheeled it to the front of the courtroom. Mr. Dinkle picked up a portable tape player.

"I'd like you to identify the contents of this box," he said. He clicked on the tape player and cheerful circus music began playing.

"Da, Da, Da, Da, Da, Da. Ta-Da!"

Suddenly, the top of the box flew open and out popped Phillip's father, Leo Laugh-a-Lot, in a gust of cotton-candy–scented air. His bright clothing colored the courtroom like melted candles on a cake.

"Happy birthday to you," Leo sang. "Happy birthday to—" He stopped. "Hey, this isn't a birthday party. What am I doing in a courtroom?" His red-painted smile belied his downturned lips. "What's going on here?"

The spectators burst into laughter. Judge Monn whacked

her gavel. "Now see here," she said to Mr. Dinkle. "What kind of mischief is this? What is this clown doing in my courtroom? You had better have a good explanation."

"Maybe Mr. Stanislaw would like to explain who this clown is," said Mr. Dinkle, pointing at Phillip. "How about it?"

Phillip's jaw hung open like the lid on a broken trunk. Leo spotted him on the witness stand.

"Phillip?" Leo asked. "What are you doing here?" He heaved himself out and landed on his rump. His clown suit's built-in rump protector made a loud toot.

Phillip felt his ears catch fire.

"Someone explain what's going on," Judge Monn demanded. "Tipstaff, remove this clown from the courtroom!"

The tipstaff helped Leo to his feet and began leading him out of the courtroom. Phillip didn't know if he was taking him back to the lobby, back to the circus, or off to jail. He thought about his dad in the Hardingtown County lockup next to criminals with names like "Bruiser" and "Mad Dog."

"Wait!" yelled Phillip. "Don't."

They froze: the reporters with their pencils posed over notebooks, the townspeople, his classmates—immobilized like a crowd watching a performer pry open the mouth of a lion. Waiting. Breathless. For what would happen next.

"That clown," said Phillip, "is my dad."

The news rolled across the crowd like a storm, growing from a murmur, to a rumble, to a full-pitched thunder that filled the room. Mouths went wild with excited jabbering. A frail woman in a pastel church dress gasped and pressed her hand to her heart. Her husband, in a silky button-down shirt and necktie, fell out of his seat. A rough-skinned man in a flannel shirt and suspenders nearly lost his dentures. Reporters scribbled frantically on bent pads as they tried to catch individual quotes amid the roar.

Leo bowed and curtsied like the featured act in a one-clown show. He pulled an endless stream of handkerchiefs from the tipstaff's shirt pocket. He honked his rump protector and tossed colorful birthday streamers into the audience.

Kids in the back row whipped their heads from side to side in violent fits of laughter. Phillip wasn't sure if they were laughing at his father or at him. Then he saw something that made him realize it didn't matter. His friends—a girl whom he had helped with her reading, a boy whom he had shared his lunch with, another boy whose books he had helped pick up in the school hallway, and all the kids who were the easy dodgeball targets—they weren't laughing. They were clapping. And smiling. At him.

Shawn put his index finger and thumb in his mouth and blew them like a whistle. Then he held a thumbs-up to Phillip.

Phillip leaned back in his chair and relaxed. No matter what happened next, he knew he wouldn't have to hide who he was or where he came from ever again.

"You will come to order," Judge Monn tried to yell above the ruckus. But even she could not calm the spectators.

Leo hit a button on his neck strap and his bow tie spun.

Judge Monn threw her useless gavel over her shoulder and stood up. "In my chambers!" she ordered the lawyers as she stomped off. "And bring that clown with you."

27

Judges are a lot like circus balloons. As he stood before Judge Monn in her chambers, Phillip thought: You can fill them full of hot air, but if you go too far, they'll explode.

"This man," Leo said, grabbing Mr. Dinkle. "This man said he was hiring me to perform at a birthday party. He had me get into the box and told me not to jump out until I heard the *Ta-Da!*"

"Not a birthday party," said Mr. Dinkle. "A surprise party."

"I just wanted to earn a few bucks and get a free trip to Hardingtown to visit my boy," said Leo.

"Surprise party, my foot!" Judge Monn said to Mr. Dinkle. "How dare you turn my courtroom into a three-ring circus." Mr. Dinkle and his assistants looked more like guilty school-children than lawyers.

"One ring."

"What was that?" asked the Judge.

"It was me," said Phillip, stepping to the front of the group and speaking more like a lawyer than a schoolboy. "A three-ring circus has three performances going on at the same time. The rings are—"

"Your Honor," said Mr. Dinkle. "If I might be permitted to speak."

Judge Monn shook her head and raised her hand.

"No. That's enough. I'm putting my foot down. Mr. Dinkle, I ought to cite you for contempt of court for that stunt you pulled out there. Even if you win this case, what will it look like? A big factory with high-priced lawyers beating a little kid. And for what? For the price of a pair of eyeglasses. When I practiced law, we didn't try cases like this. Why haven't you settled?"

"Well," said Mr. Dinkle, "it's not only the money. The plaintiff has accused the factory of creating a dangerous product. To be fair, we have to defend ourselves."

"Do you think what you did out there in my courtroom with Bozo the clown was being fair?" asked Judge Monn.

"Leo," said Phillip. "His name is not Bozo. It's Leo Laugh-a-Lot."

Phillip's father adjusted his buzzer and put his hand out to shake the judge's hand. "Pleased to meet you, Your Highness," he said. Phillip pushed his father's hand down.

"The only reason I let this case go forward," Judge Monn advised Phillip, "was because I wanted to teach you a lesson about filing frivolous lawsuits. I should have dismissed it from the start."

"We agree entirely, Your Honor," a gloating Mr. Dinkle said.

"Kick that smile off your face," said Judge Monn. "The point is that this case should be settled." She stood up, took off her robe, and hung it on a hook. "It's a quarter past twelve now. We will adjourn for lunch and resume at one-thirty. When I return, I expect to hear that the parties have found a way to resolve their differences."

"Shall we shake on it?" Leo asked.

Judge Monn pressed papers into her briefcase and headed for the door. "We should not be wasting valuable court time on this matter," she said. As if to emphasize the conviction of her feelings, the door rattled behind her.

"What do we do now?" Phillip asked Sam.

"You heard the judge," Sam said. "We settle the case."

The dodgeball lawyers left and returned with Mr. Nerp and Coach. B.B. stood in the doorway waiting for her father. She slid off one of her high-heeled shoes and rubbed her foot. Leo went over and began pulling coins from behind her ears. Finally, the dodgeball lawyers broke from their huddle.

"Two hundred and forty-nine dollars. That's the offer," said Mr. Dinkle.

"Would I get the injunction to stop the school from forcing us to play dodgeball?" asked Phillip.

"No," said Mr. Dinkle. "The offer is for two hundred and forty-nine dollars. Take it or leave it."

Phillip felt like a kid with a piece of candy that had fallen on a dirty floor; he was unsure what to do. On the one hand, he wanted to get the money to pay back Aunt Veola. On the other hand, if he settled only for the money, there would be more dodgeball games and more broken glasses. It had taken Phillip a long time to get people to start thinking about whether dodgeball was an unsafe sport; if he took the money, they would all stop thinking.

"Look, kid," said Ms. Jones. "You're not going to win anyway. Two hundred and forty-nine dollars is better than nothing."

"Yes," agreed Mr. Terry, Mr. Dinkle's other assistant. "Don't get greedy. It's better to have a piece of a donut than to have the whole donut hole."

Phillip asked Coach, "Would we still have to play dodgeball every day in gym class?"

"Of course," said Coach. "How else could we train for the dodgeball tournament?"

"Would you still try to cream me all the time?" he asked B.B.

She hesitated.

"Of course she would try to get you out," said Coach. "She's the best junior dodgeballer in Hardingtown."

Phillip looked at Sam. He was as still as an acrobat waiting for his cue.

"Sam, what do you think I should do?"

"Why are you asking me?" Sam crossed his arms. "For that matter, why are you asking Mr. Dinkle or Mr. Tyson or B.B. what they think? Only you know what you're willing to settle for."

"You're right," Phillip said. "I do know." He climbed onto a chair.

"Here is what I want," Phillip said. "Mr. Nerp, I want you to have your factory make your dodgeballs softer so they won't hurt kids when they get hit."

"Don't be absurd," said Mr. Nerp.

"B.B., I want you to promise you won't try to hurt anyone smaller than you, even when you're really mad. And Coach, I want you to allow optional sports during gym class. Safe sports for kids who don't want to spend their childhoods as human targets."

"You're way out of line, Stanislaw," said Coach.

"Finally, Mr. Dinkle, I want you to apologize to my dad for tricking him into coming here."

"Who do you think you are, making such demands?"

asked Mr. Dinkle. He glared at Phillip with flaming dodge-ball eyes.

"Who do I think I am?" Phillip asked himself out loud. He hesitated, wondering how he could make them understand.

"Nobody special," he said finally. He smoothed down the tuft of red hair that stuck up on the back of his head and took a deep breath. "I am Phillip Edward Stanislaw. Son of Leo Laugh-a-Lot and Matilda the Fat Lady, nephew of Veola the security guard and Felix the cargo loader. I can scoop poop almost faster than an elephant can make it and can juggle four dodgeballs, maybe five, but I haven't tried that yet. I'm just a regular kid. But even a regular kid knows it's wrong to let big kids hurt little kids, and somebody's got to do something about it." His glasses slid down his nose, and he pushed them back up.

"You're insane," said Coach. He grabbed B.B. by the arm and stormed out of the room. Mr. Nerp nodded in agreement. "Nothing. That's what you'll be getting. Not a single penny. We are going to beat your pants off in court."

"Pants?" said Leo. "What a great idea." He searched the pockets of his baggy trousers, pulled out a unicycle horn, and chased Mr. Dinkle and the others out of the room with rude honking sounds.

When only he and Sam were left, Phillip realized his right hand was pointed in the air like the Statue of Liberty. He scampered down from the chair, thinking about the $249 he could have had if he had been willing to drop the lawsuit.

"Are you okay?" Sam asked.

"I'd rather be a loser than a quitter," said Phillip.

"Keep your chin up," Sam said. "You haven't lost yet."

28

A circus clown named Joseph was so successful that it became popular to call all clowns Joey. Phillip wondered, if he lost his lawsuit, would people start to call all losers Phillip?

"I'm going to the snack bar to get a bite," said Sam. "Want to come?" When his lawsuit had begun, Phillip had hungered for justice. Now he would be happy with a ham sandwich.

"No. Thanks," said Phillip, ignoring his grumbling stomach. He needed to use the time to think of a way to get the settlement he wanted. But how? After Sam left, Phillip went to the courtroom and sat in Judge Monn's chair. He tried to look at things like a judge would. Then he went over and sat in Mr. Dinkle's chair and then in Mr. Nerp's chair.

"Your mom would take away my rubber chicken if she found out I let you skip a meal."

Phillip swung around in the chair. His dad was holding a take-out box from the snack bar. In it was a dodgeballburger, a root beer, a bag of chips, and two packets of ketchup. Leo set it on the defendants' table and scratched a spot on his huge red nose.

"Thanks, Dad."

"Hold your horses," said Leo. He strained his face, reached in his giant trouser pocket, and pulled out a bag of cotton candy.

"It got a little smashed when I sat on it while I was in the exhibit box."

Phillip opened the bag and breathed in the memories. He picked off a piece of the pink fluff and tasted it. It melted on his tongue.

"Veola filled me in on how all this lawsuit stuff got started," said Leo.

"Coach says I'm insane for trying to stop dodgeball."

"If I thought you were crazy," said Leo, "I would have sent you to clown school." He hit a button on his neck strap and his bow tie spun. "Oops, what time is it?" Leo checked the clock. "I've got to call your mom and let her know what's going on." He rushed for the door. "Bump a nose," he called on his way out.

Phillip wished his dad had stayed longer. He began thinking about how much he missed his mom. He really did love his parents. No matter how old you get, he thought, there are times when you could use a hug from your mom or dad. This was one of those times.

The ticking of the wall clock was the only sound in the room. It was nearly 1:15 already. They would be back soon, and he still hadn't figured out how to get the settlement he wanted.

Phillip had read about old-fashioned ways used to determine who won a court case. Using the "trial by morsel" method, the accused would be forced to swallow a chunk of cheese. If it got stuck in his throat and he died, he lost. When

Phillip first read about this, he found it barbaric. But even choking on mold now seemed more pleasant than facing off with Mr. Dinkle again.

Phillip wandered over to a large window and looked down. The courtroom was on the second floor, but there were no obstructions and he had a clear view to the street below. A news crew was set up off to the side of the courthouse steps, probably waiting to talk to the parties as they came back from lunch recess. The kids from his school were sitting on the steps, still finishing their brown-bag lunches. Judge Monn was talking to one of Phillip's teachers.

A telephone booth was on the sidewalk across from the courthouse. Phillip could see a brightly clothed person inside. He figured it was probably his dad calling his mom.

Mr. Dinkle and Mr. Nerp were walking past the phone booth, with Coach, B.B., and Mr. Dinkle's assistants a few yards behind them. Vice-principal Race was there, too. The news anchor and cameraman sped over to them. Mr. Dinkle appeared to be giving a speech. He had one arm around Mr. Nerp's shoulder and the other around Mr. Race's shoulder. He wore a confident smile. As he watched them, it occurred to Phillip that they had probably never been hit by dodgeballs in their lives. He pictured the men as young boys out in the woods hunting bunnies with double-barreled guns.

"Phillip, are you still here?" Sam's voice brought Phillip back to reality.

"I'm over at the window."

"Don't jump," Sam joked. Phillip turned around and rolled his eyes. He swatted at what sounded like a nearby fly.

"What is that?" Sam asked.

"What is what?"

"That sound," said Sam. Phillip swatted again at the buzzing. Then he realized there was no fly.

"It sounds like an airplane," said Sam. "But there's something more to it." Phillip pressed his face against the window and looked as high up as he could. He saw a small cargo plane overhead. It was flying low, like it had recently taken off. The airplane's cargo door was flapping in the wind.

"It's a plane," said Phillip. "But it looks like something is falling out of it." He strained to see what it was. It looked like bits of confetti. Hundreds, maybe thousands, of pieces of . . .

"What is it?" asked Sam.

"It looks like . . . dodgeballs."

"Dodgeballs? Falling out of an airplane? Are you serious?"

Phillip looked down at the crowd of people in front of the courthouse. "They're gonna get creamed," he yelled. "I've got to warn them." He tried frantically to open the window. "It's stuck tight."

"I'll get the window," said Sam as he felt for the wall. "You get down there and get those people out of the way."

Phillip had never felt his feet fly before. They seemed to take off before his brain even had time to send the message. He took the steps three at a time, bounding like a hurdle racer, then zipped through the corridor. This was impossible. It couldn't be happening. Dodgeballs don't fall out of the sky. As he pushed through the heavy glass doors, he could hear Sam's deep voice thunder through the open window.

"Look out belooooowwwwwwww!"

A small girl pointed skyward as the rubber cannonballs plummeted toward the earth. Phillip cupped his hands around his mouth.

"Run for your lives!" he shouted, but his words were swallowed by the sounds of screaming men, women, and children already bolting for cover.

Soda cans, backpacks, and briefcases dropped like sweat. Panicked bodies sprinted up the courthouse steps to the safety of a canopy leading to the entry doors. The rush of terrified schoolchildren nearly knocked Phillip over. It was all he could do to keep from being pushed back into the courthouse by the fleeing crowd.

Like the first few kernels in a bag of microwave popcorn, balls began to explode against the streets and buildings. Below the steps, the television cameraman continued to film. A dodgeball rewarded him for his arrogance with a wham in the derriere that sent him and his camera flying in different directions. The ball ricocheted off a mailbox and returned. It hit the camera dead center, as if aiming, and destroyed the evidence of its bad behavior.

Judge Monn, who was close to the top of the steps, began running toward the injured cameraman. A screamer nearly got her, then another, forcing her to flee back up the steps and dive for the relative safety of the canopy. Phillip fought his way through the current of rushing children. He caught a glimpse of B.B., trapped in an open area. She and Coach, along with Mr. Terry and Ms. Jones, had stopped to help the fallen cameraman. There was nowhere for them to go and no time to get there.

Suddenly, the door to the phone booth flew open, and Leo jumped out. Phillip wanted to yell for him to stay inside, but deafening thuds and crashes would have made it futile.

Mr. Dinkle had somehow made it past the airborne land mines and across the street. He was fleeing up the steps, holding his arm. Mr. Nerp was close behind. As Mr. Dinkle got near the top, a ball slammed into his left leg. His wounded howl rose above the chaos. Judge Monn ran out and grabbed him by his good arm and began pulling him to safety. Phillip helped her pull. Mr. Dinkle slid up the last of the steps on his belly.

It was hard to see through the rain of dodgeballs. The merciless spheres were hitting the ground and ricocheting off buildings from every conceivable angle. Phillip ducked as a ball sailed straight for him. With a flagrant lack of judicial decorum, the shameless ball creamed Judge Monn in the face. She dropped to the ground.

Aunt Veola and another security guard appeared with a first-aid kit and helped Judge Monn sit up. With gloved hands, Aunt Veola pulled out some thick gauze and pressed it against the judge's head.

"Help me!" Mr. Nerp sobbed as he crawled up the steps. Aunt Veola lifted Judge Monn's hand to make her hold the gauze to her head.

"Hold this here," she instructed the judge. She and the other guard raced to help Mr. Nerp.

Judge Monn began to teeter backward. Her pupils rolled behind her eyelids. Phillip slipped his lap under her head just as it was about to meet the concrete and applied pressure to her wound. As he strained to see if B.B. had made it to safety, he witnessed something amazing.

His dad, darting between balls as only a well-trained cir-cus clown can, was helping a stunned Mr. Race into the safety of the phone booth. In a flash of bright-colored cloth-ing, Leo ran over to Coach, who had the cameraman slung over his broad shoulder, and pushed them into the booth, too. One by one, he plucked the remaining people from danger—B.B., Mr. Terry, Ms. Jones—and squashed them into the burgeoning booth. Then he expertly pressed himself into the already overstuffed space and, using all of the rushing adrenaline inside him, yanked the door shut. Completely shut.

The balls were coming down with full force now, going every which way, like elbow macaroni boiling in a pot on the stove. Phillip leaned his body over the judge to give her as much cover as possible and repeated a prayer that Bartholomew the Giant had taught him. Judge Monn, still only semiconscious, began mumbling along.

When the roar of impacting balls finally subsided, Phillip looked up. The glass was covered with spiderweb cracks, but the phone booth was still standing. Slowly, the door cracked open and seven dazed occupants spilled out.

The judge moaned.

"What happened?" she asked Phillip.

"He did it," said Phillip proudly. "After all these years. My dad stuffed more than six clowns into a telephone booth."

29

Victor the Voracious Fire-eater tried three times to teach Phillip's dad how to swallow fire. The first time, Leo burned his tongue. The second time, Leo got frostbite on his tongue from the ice he used to prevent a burn. The third time, Leo got a severe stomachache from accidentally swallowing the bandage he had secured around his tongue to prevent burning and freezing. Nonetheless, as Phillip looked around at the injured lawyers in Judge Monn's office the next morning, he wondered if fire-eating might be safer than lawyering.

Judge Monn's chambers looked like a hospital ward. Her eyes were swollen, and she had a patch on her head covering six stitches. Mr. Dinkle had his left leg in a cast and right arm in a sling. Coach had a bandage on his nose, which had been smashed against the phone booth. Ms. Jones, Mr. Nerp, Mr. Terry, and B.B. appeared to have sustained no physical injury, although Ms. Jones's skin seemed two shades lighter than it had been the day before.

Mr. Race, who was still being treated for shock at Hardingtown Memorial Hospital, was not in attendance.

"Ouch! That must have really hurt," Phillip said when he saw Judge Monn.

"Darn right, young man," she said, her voice shaking, "and I assure you, it still does."

"But not as much as the class-action lawsuit that I'm bringing against the Hardingtown Airport for dropping that load is going to hurt the people responsible for this disaster," said Mr. Dinkle. "I'm assuming Your Honor will want to sue the airport, too?"

"You don't get it, do you, Mr. Dinkle?" Judge Monn asked. His expression confirmed her suspicion.

"I believe things happen for a reason," Judge Monn said. "Some higher power made that shipment of dodgeballs from the factory fall out of the airplane cargo hold at that exact moment in time. He, or She, was trying to tell us something. I intend to listen."

Mr. Dinkle stared at her as if she had lost her mind.

"Those dodgeballs didn't just knock my socks off," she continued. "They knocked some sense into me. Mr. Stanislaw, you and I may have gotten off on the wrong foot. But, given recent events, I can understand why you would think a dodgeball is an unreasonably unsafe product. I am inclined to agree."

"But, Your Honor," Mr. Dinkle began.

"There are no buts," said Judge Monn. "The only question is what to do about it."

Phillip put his hand up. "I have a suggestion," he said. "Maybe if the balls were softer, they wouldn't hurt so much."

"How about it, Mr. Nerp?" asked Judge Monn. "Have you considered making softer balls?"

Mr. Nerp straightened himself to a standing position. His bloodshot eyes shifted around the room. "A vinyl-coated, foam-rubber ball would be softer, but it would cost more," he said. "Switching to foam-ball production couldn't happen overnight. There would be lag time while we retool." His eyes darted to a crack in the ceiling, as if he expected it to burst open so dodgeballs could continue the prior day's assault. "But all things considered, we might be willing to do it."

"Excellent," said Judge Monn. She turned to Coach. "Until the new balls are in production, perhaps you could play something else in gym class."

"The kids have to practice," said Coach.

"What if," asked Phillip, "you let the dodgeballers practice, but let the other kids play a different sport?"

"I can't supervise two sports at once," said Coach.

"Any other suggestions?" asked Judge Monn. She learned back in her chair and beat her fingers against her desk. B.B. raised her hand.

"Maybe if Dad had an assistant," said B.B., "we could have regular dodgeball and an alternative sport."

"Do you have someone in mind?" asked Judge Monn.

"Yes," she said, "Phillip." He looked at her in astonishment.

"I don't know how to play any sports," Phillip said.

"Yes, you do," said B.B. "You can juggle." The group turned to Coach for his response. He adjusted the bandage on his nose.

"Technically," Coach admitted, "I suppose juggling is a sport."

"It's settled, then," said Judge Monn. "Phillip can teach an alternative class of juggling for kids who don't wish to participate in dodgeball. Is everyone satisfied by the terms of the settlement?"

Phillip removed a piece of paper from his pocket. It listed

his settlement terms. "There are a couple things that are missing, Your Honor," he said.

Judge Monn leaned back in her chair again.

"First," said Phillip, "I would like the school to adopt the rules used by the National Amateur Dodgeball Association, which prohibits head shots."

"I can live with that," said Coach.

"Second," said Phillip, "I still need to pay Aunt Veola the two hundred and forty-nine dollars for my new glasses."

"Who's willing to foot the bill?" asked Judge Monn.

"I'll take care of it," said Mr. Nerp.

"No, I'll pay for it," said Coach. "I'm the one who forced him to play."

"But I'm the one who creamed him," said B.B. "I should pay. If it's okay for me to pay a little at a time."

"How about ten dollars a week?" Phillip asked.

"I can live with that," B.B. said.

Phillip told the judge there was one last issue, and when they were done working out the details of it, Judge Monn picked up a tape recorder and immortalized the terms of the settlement. When she said they were adjourned, they started shaking hands and saying good-bye.

B.B. asked Phillip if he would come over to her house sometime to teach her juggling, since she was still probably going to take dodgeball in gym class, and Coach said it would be okay. Judge Monn gave Phillip a big hug and thanked him for having such a comfortable lap.

Mr. Nerp told Phillip he ought to consider a career in the law. Mr. Terry and Ms. Jones, and even Mr. Dinkle, agreed and said if he ever needed a recommendation to get into law school he should call their firm.

Hardest of all was shaking hands with Sam, because trying to tell him how much he had helped made Phillip stumble over the words.

"Don't thank me," said Sam. "You're the one who did it."

"But you believed in me," said Phillip. "Even when I didn't believe in myself."

"That's what friends are for," said Sam. "Remember our deal?"

"Anytime you need someone to share your problems with, you come see me," Phillip said.

"That's right. And anytime you need me, I'll be there for you. It all evens out in the end."

He extended his hand and Phillip shook it for a long time. The whole thing was terribly serious until the group wandered out into the hallway, and Phillip's dad heard the good news.

"Put it there, son," Leo said. Phillip shook without thinking.

Bzzzzz. His dad's buzzer made Phillip's whole hand tingle.

They all laughed—even Phillip. Not because he thought the gag was funny. Phillip laughed because it felt good having his circus dad and his legal friends share a joke.

The real world is like a dodgeball game, Phillip realized. A place where, as his dad said, it's better to have your eye on the ball than a ball in your eye. Some people scramble to survive, others fight to win. If Phillip became a lawyer when he grew up, he could help people learn to get along and play by the rules.

At the same time, Phillip didn't want to give up his circus life entirely. He actually missed the circus. Not the banana-cream pies. But lots of other things, like hearing the relief of a crowd when an acrobat makes it safely to a platform and watching the quiet dignity of Bartholemew the Giant when he rides on Einstein the elephant. The circus was still a part of him, and it always would be.

He wouldn't just become a lawyer, he would become a circus-law lawyer.

But how would he tell his dad? After all, becoming a circus-law lawyer wasn't exactly a regular thing to do, and he had made such a fuss about wanting to be a regular kid. Wasn't that why his mom had sent him to live in Hardingtown to begin with?

"Regular?" asked Leo as he and Phillip waited for Aunt Veola to bring her car around. "Is there such a thing?" Phillip expected his dad to toot his horn or spin his bow tie, but he didn't. He was serious.

"I know about the Dodgeball Cheerleader Fiasco," Phillip said. "Sam told me."

"Did he tell you what happened after the fiasco?"

Phillip shook his head.

"Your mother ran away from Hardingtown that day," said Leo. "Ran away because she felt she didn't fit in. Really, she was trying to run away from herself, because she didn't think she would ever fit in anywhere. I'm not sure how she got the circus ticket and ended up at the afternoon matinee in Kansas City the next week. She was still upset about what Stinky did. When one of the clowns threw a bucket of confetti on her, she got so mad she chased him around the ring."

"Did she catch him?" Phillip asked.

"Almost," said Leo. "He jumped into the tiger cage for protection. The audience thought it was part of the show. They loved it. When Matilda realized they were clapping for her, she took a bow. The Windy Van Hooten Circus signed her to a contract before the third act, and she was learning how to juggle flaming arrows the next day. She was the most beautiful thing I had ever seen."

Phillip felt his eyes tearing up. He was proud of his mom for having the courage to find her place in the world. Leo used his sleeve to wipe his own eyes. The greasepaint left a white streak on his costume. They stood in silence, faces to the wind.

"Maybe that's what I was doing," Phillip said finally. "When I wanted to get away from the circus. Trying to run away from myself."

Leo smiled. "I thought maybe you were trying to run away from me." He slapped his hand against his rump protector and gave off a loud *toot*. Then he got serious again. "All those years I wasted trying to find a circus act you could do to make you great," Leo said. "I was a fool. You've been stupendous since the day you were born."

Phillip grabbed Leo and hugged him with all his might. Leo squeezed him back, ferociously, more like a lion tamer than a clown. They didn't stop hugging until they heard Aunt Veola's horn.

"One more thing," said Leo right before they got in the car. He motioned for Phillip to lean in close. Then he squirted him in the nose with his water-flower pin.

"Gotcha!" his dad said. He hit the button on his neck strap, and his bow tie spun.

30

Most people have heard the expression "Elephants never forget," but exactly what is it that an elephant needs to remember?

The next morning, when Phillip rolled over in his bed at Aunt Veola's house, he was awakened to the sound of his cheek hitting a whoopee cushion. A note on it said, "Come down for a breakfast surprise." Phillip crept down the stairs slowly, listening carefully for the low growl of bears or tigers. The smell of fried bacon drifted from the kitchen.

"He's going to be late for school if he doesn't get up soon," he heard Aunt Veola say.

"Give him five more minutes," said a softer voice.

Phillip tripped down the last three steps and landed in a heap at the bottom. That voice! Could it be?

"Mom?" asked Phillip.

A figure filled the kitchen doorway so fully it dimmed the light to the hall.

"Surprise!" yelled Matilda. She pulled him up and squeezed him against her giant polka-dot dress. It felt so good to see his mom again, he didn't even care if he suffocated.

"Did you hear about the lawsuit?" he asked when she finally released him.

"I'm so proud of you," she said.

That's when he remembered.

"Wait," he said. He rushed to the front door, scooped up the morning newspaper, and raced back. "I have something for you."

Matilda slid the paper out of its plastic cover and removed the rubber band. She unrolled it and read the headline: FACTORY TO RETOOL FOR SOFTER BALL PRODUCTION.

"No," said Phillip excitedly. He grabbed the paper and shuffled the pages, searching. "Down there."

In the lower right corner was a boxed article that had a copy of a handwritten letter. At the top of the article it said, in extra-large, bold black letters: **STINKY TELLS ALL**.

"I think I'm going to faint," Matilda said. Phillip helped her to the kitchen and pulled out two chairs so she could sit. The table was covered with plates full of fluffy pancakes, maple sausages, and curly tangles of bacon. Aunt Veola was buttering a warm stack of toast. Uncle Felix and Leo were shoveling scoops of slippery scrambled eggs into their mouths. When they saw Matilda's stunned expression, they all stopped.

"What is it?" asked Leo.

Phillip cleared a space and set the newspaper in front of her. "Go ahead," he said. Matilda picked the paper up by its edges. It shook softly as she read.

Dear Matilda,

I am sorry for hitting you with a dodgeball on the day of the Regional High School Championship game fourteen years ago. It was my fault you dropped the cheerleaders. I promise to never bully anyone ever again.

Yours truly,

Ernest P. ("Stinky") Race

The newspaper drifted to the table. "How did you . . . How could you . . ." Her eyes got drippy and her voice got squeaky and she couldn't get all the words out. Aunt Veola reached over and held her sister's hand.

"It was the last part of the settlement," said Phillip. "I asked the judge to make Mr. Race write a letter of apology as soon as he came out of shock. I said to give the letter to Shawn so he could give it to his grandfather's dentist's brother. He's a reporter."

"After all these years," said Matilda. "I can hardly believe it." Even Uncle Felix was speechless.

Matilda picked the paper back up and reread the article. "Hold on, there's more. I missed a line." She read the final sentence, the one underneath Stinky's signature: "'P.S. Could we keep this apology our little secret?'"

"Oops," said Leo.

Dong Ding, announced Aunt Veola's doorbell, which Uncle Felix had installed himself.

"It better not be that pesky vacuum-cleaner salesman," said Aunt Veola.

"I'll get it," said Phillip.

He grabbed the knob and threw the door open.

"Hey," said B.B. A backpack was slung over her gray wool jacket. "Are you going to school, or what? I usually ride with my dad, but we just live a couple of blocks from you, so I figured maybe I'd try walking today."

"With me?"

"You got a problem with that?"

"No," said Phillip. "Want to come in while I get dressed?"

"Okay," she said.

"Tell him I already have a vacuum cleaner," Aunt Veola yelled.

"It's not a salesman, it's . . . a friend."

"Was that your mom?" asked B.B.

"No," said Phillip. "That was my aunt. My mom is . . ." He almost said the fat lady. "Matilda. She's in the kitchen." Phillip led B.B. to the kitchen.

"This is my mother," he said.

"Hello," said Matilda.

"Nice to meet you," said B.B.

"She can juggle flaming arrows," Phillip said.

"Wow," said B.B. "That's really cool."

Phillip slipped upstairs and threw his school clothes on while his parents entertained B.B. with circus stories. As he was coming downstairs, he heard the doorbell again.

"I'll get it," he yelled. It was Shawn.

"Did you see the letter?" Shawn asked as he let himself in.

Phillip nodded. "Thanks for your help."

"No problem, buddy. Can you believe it? They used to call him Stinky. He's gonna have to transfer to a different district. I mean, who's gonna be afraid of a vice-principal named Stinky?"

Phillip took Shawn into the kitchen and introduced him. "Shawn is the one who warned me about the kids who wanted to put me out of commission during the dodgeball game," he said.

"Don't give me all the credit," said Shawn as he accepted a pancake and sausage from Matilda. "I was just passing along what B.B. told me." Phillip saw a vision of B.B. in the gym trying to retreat as the kids whose parents worked at the factory began their four-ball assault.

"That's why they were after you," Phillip said. "They found out you warned me. Since they couldn't get me, they went after you."

B.B. shrugged. "It was no big deal."

"Can I get more pancakes and sausage?" Shawn asked.

Matilda put two sausages in a jumbo-size pancake, rolled it up, and handed it to him. "Better take it to go," she said.

"And tell your parents you're invited here tomorrow for Thanksgiving dinner," added Aunt Veola. "We'll be having a big turkey."

The air outside was brisk. It made their breath pour out like steam. As they walked, they talked about ordinary things, like why school cafeteria food is so bad and why dividing fractions is so hard.

They walked past the smokestack to Mr. Nerp's factory, where the neon letters proudly announced it was still the American Dodgeball Company. They strolled past Friendly's Gas-'n-Go, where the old couple, snuggled on the bench with a thick blanket across their laps, waved to them. They stopped at the window of Newman's Trophy shop to argue about how tall the giant silver statue in the window really was. They laughed at the hopelessly mangled, red-taped eyeglasses that were displayed in a special case in the front window of the optical shop under a sign that asked: TIME FOR A REPLACEMENT PAIR? Finally, they turned the corner and passed the Hardingtown County Courthouse, where an eleven-year-old boy had made dodgeball history.

As they approached the Hardingtown Middle School, Shawn said, "Maybe someday I'll join the circus."

"You?" asked B.B. "What could you do?"

"I could be the fat boy."

"There's no such thing as a fat boy," said B.B. "Just a fat man and a fat lady."

"That doesn't seem fair," said Shawn. "Maybe I'll have to change that. I could be the world's first circus fat boy."

Phillip smiled. "Why not?" he said.

"What about you?" B.B. asked Phillip. "Are you going to stay in Hardingtown, or do you have to go back to the circus?"

"My parents said I could stay if I want to," said Phillip.

"Do you want to?" asked Shawn.

In his mind's eye, Phillip could see a circus boy shoveling horse poop, a hunk of popcorn-covered caramel apple stuck in his hair, yearning for something more out of life.

"Yes," he said, "I'd like to stay." His answer came out effortlessly and formed a little cloud that looked like it could hang in the air forever.

As they were about to enter the school, B.B. stopped them. "I still have one question," she said. "Why *did* those dodgeballs fall out of the sky?" The three looked to the heavens, as if the answer would appear there. But it didn't.

All through the school day, Phillip thought about it. Maybe Judge Monn was right. Maybe it was some higher power that made the airplane suddenly lose its shipment of dodgeballs. What else could it have been?

When they arrived home that night, Uncle Felix was sitting on the front porch.

He had gotten fired from his job as a cargo loader at the airport for forgetting to latch the airplane's cargo door.

Turn the page for a peek at
Janice Repka's next book:

brains, meet beauty.

the
clueless
girl's
guide
to being a
genius

Janice Repka

AUTHOR OF
*The Stupendous
Dodgeball Fiasco*

1   Aphrodite Wigglesmith
Gets It Started

ere's something fun you can do. First, get out of your chair. (I'm trusting you on that.) Next, stand in an open space. (Trusting you again.) Now spin like a quantum mechanical particle. (Or a top or tornado, whatever.) Faster. Faster. STOP. Did you feel it? That slip-in-time moment when your brain hadn't caught up with your body and it felt like you were still spinning? I love that. It's like my body has outsmarted my brain, which is not easy to do. Excuse the pun, but my brain kind of has a mind of its own. If you put a math problem, no matter how hard, in front of my eyes it sets off this switch and I have to try to solve it. So my life's been a little weird, I guess you could say.

The weirdness started the day someone flushed a firecracker down a toilet in the boys' bathroom on the second floor of Carnegie Middle School. The potty shattered, a weak pipe burst, and sewage water rained into the school office below.

"Holy crap!" Principal DeGuy yelled to his secretary. "Get someone here fast."

My mother, Cecelia Wigglesmith, was the "plumber on call" that day. She loaded crescent wrenches and extra piping into her truck while I climbed into my car seat. Although only four years old, I was already a mini-version of my mother physically—petite, with pale skin and black hair. But intellectually, I was bored silly and hungering for stimulation. To keep busy on the way to the plumbing job, I counted each church we passed on the left and each bar we passed on the right and kept a working ratio.

A few miles later, a sign announced we had reached Carnegie Middle School, "home to the division champion wrestling team, the Carnegie Spiders." The school was ten times as long as my house and five times as wide. Inside the office, Mother set me down on a desk.

"You stay here while I find the shutoff valve," she said. She turned to the secretary. "I hope you don't mind keeping an eye on my daughter. I'll be back as soon as things are under control."

The secretary was also perched on top of a desk. She was wearing a flamingo pink dress and held up her right foot. Her right shoe, which must have dropped when she hopped up, was floating out the door. The smell alone would have reduced most four-year-olds to tears, but to me, it just smelled like Mother had come home from work.

After Mother left, a piece of soaked ceiling tile fell and splattered us with sewage water. The secretary screamed and I jumped. The office phones began to ring. I counted the number of rings. I counted the number of ceiling chunks that fell and the number of times we screamed and jumped. I found that: 5 rings + 1 splash = 1 scream + 1 jump.

"You've got a shattered toilet and a burst pipe in the boys' bathroom," Mother said when she returned.

"Can you fix it?" asked Principal DeGuy, following her. He was middle-aged, but most of his hair hadn't made it that far. What was left covered his lower head in a U-shape. "We're scheduled for state testing in the morning, so I can't cancel school tomorrow."

"Once the pipe's repaired, I'll have to bail," said Mother. "Pumps will only pull so many gallons per hour. You've got four inches of water on the first floor, eighteen in the basement. Goodness knows how long that could take."

"Three hours and twenty-five minutes," I said.

Despite his ample ears, Principal DeGuy did not seem to hear. "I'm not interested in what goodness knows," he told Mother. "How long will *you* need to get this water out?"

"Three hours and twenty-five minutes," I repeated.

"Whose child is this?"

Mother picked me up and held me against her hip. "She's mine. Do you have a calculator?" Principal De-Guy pulled out his computerized planner. Mother told him the formula to figure out how long it would take.

"Three hours and twenty-five minutes," he said.

They stared at me.

"How did you do that?" Mother asked.

I shrugged and counted the number of teeth in the principal's open mouth.

"You gave her the answer," he said.

"I'm sure it was just a coincidence," Mother replied. "Aphrodite is usually so quiet you don't know she's in the room."

A chunk of ceiling tile fell and splashed Principal DeGuy with water. The secretary screamed again.

"I'd better get those pumps started. Would you

mind?" Mother handed me to the principal and splashed her way out. He set me on a desk.

"How many polka dots are on my tie?" he asked.

I used my method for counting cereal boxes at the supermarket, the number up multiplied by the number sideways. Then I took some away because of the funny shape at the bottom of the necktie. "One hundred and fifty seven," I answered.

Principal DeGuy hopped onto the desk with me and emptied the water from his shoes. "Who is the queen of England?"

"I don't know."

"What is 157 multiplied by 23?"

I pushed the bangs out of my eyes. "3,611."

He ran the numbers. "Holy human calculator!"

The secretary handed him a telephone, and he dialed the number for the Office of Special and Gifted Testing. "Little lady," he told me, "if you are what I think you are, your whole world is about to change."

And, boy, did it ever. Not that I'm complaining. Once they found out my IQ was 204, they let me start school early. It was like a game to see how quickly I could pass each grade (fifth took only eight weeks and I skipped second, sixth, and tenth grades completely). But then, when I was eleven, they ran out of grades, so

I had to go away to college. Now I'm a thirteen-year-old graduate student at Harvard University.

At Harvard, everybody's brain is in overdrive all the time. So sometimes, when my brain is full of numbers and feels like it's going to explode, I slip away to an empty field on the edge of campus. Then I stretch out my arms and I spin.

2 Mindy Loft Tells It Like It Was

The reason I ramble is that I don't stay focused when I talk; at least that's what my eighth-grade English teacher told me at the beginning of this school year. So if I get a little off track, try not to get your poodle in a fluff. Anyway, if I had to pick, I'd say it all began the day that Miss Brenda shared her awful secret. I hadn't even met Aphrodite yet. I was thirteen years old and living with my mom in the apartment above her beauty shop, Tiffany's House of Beauty & Nails. We had a sign that Mom changed each week with stupid sayings like "Come on in and be a beauty, from your head to your patootie."

Mom made me help at the shop, doing gross stuff like sweeping piles of severed hair, boring stuff like re-filling the spray bottles, and a little bit of cool stuff like

9

trying out the new nail polish. At least I got an allowance. But no matter how much I got paid, there was no way I was going to be a hairstylist for the rest of my life. My dream was to be a famous baton twirler.

When she was nineteen, my mom had been first runner-up for Miss Majorette of the Greater Allegheny Valley. My dad, John Loft (God rest his soul), had been one of the judges, and they had eloped before her trophy was back from the engraver. He became her manager, and they toured all over the country in a baby blue RV with a bumper sticker that said TWIRL TILL YOUR ARMS FALL OFF.

"With my panache and your talent, we're gonna set the world on fire," he told her, and they did.

Not the whole world, maybe, but at least part of the small town of Hermanfly, Nebraska. You see, there was this stupid Hermanfly Fourth of July Spectacular Parade. Dad was in a giant firecracker costume marching next to Mom, who was twirling a fire baton. They got too close and his fuse caught fire. Mom dropped the baton and screamed for help, and some woman in the crowd pulled a pair of scissors from her purse and clipped Dad's fuse just in time. That was the good news. The bad news was that by that time

Mom's flaming baton had rolled over to a storefront, which was where they were storing the fireworks for the big show.

Most everyone ran off as soon as the fireworks started going off, but Dad sat there in his firecracker costume holding onto Mom and staring up. He said that, next to Mom, it was the most beautiful thing he had ever seen. He was so pooped from all the excitement, Mom had to help him back to their motel.

The next morning, Dad was dead.

"Weak heart," the doctor told Mom. "Surprised he made it this long with that bum ticker."

Mom said a heart as big and kind as Dad's couldn't have been defective. She blamed the whole thing on the baton. So she quit the twirling circuit, moved back to Carnegie, Pennsylvania, and opened up a hair salon. That's when I was born. Because they reminded her of Dad, Mom still displayed her twirling awards all over the shop. My favorite thing to do when I was little was to pretend a hairbrush was a baton and strike poses like the figurines on top of the trophies.

One day, when I was four, I was doing a dance I made up and twirling a broken curling iron when Miss Brenda, the owner of Miss Brenda's Baton Barn, walked in the salon. She took one look at me and said, "Really, Tiffany, you can deny it all you want, but you know that little one has baton in her blood."

That creeped me out at first because I had just seen a cartoon with a vampire in it and I thought she said "bats in her blood." Even at four, I could be stupid like that. Anyway, I kept twirling whatever I could find (a customer's umbrella, another customer's walking cane, Mom's haircutting scissors) until Mom finally gave in and let me start taking lessons at Miss Brenda's Baton Barn. I still wasn't allowed to join the Squadettes (the lame name for the Baton Barn's competitive twirling team) because those twirlers had to march in the local parades. But Mom and Miss Brenda agreed that I could get unlimited private baton lessons in exchange for Miss Brenda getting unlimited salon services.

This was actually a good deal for Miss Brenda, whose mother had passed on great skin but whose father (who had to be part werewolf) had passed on a unibrow capable of growing so thick it looked like a caterpillar napping between her eyes. Miss Brenda would go to Tiffany's House of Beauty & Nails for eyebrow waxing, and, after it was gone, I would pretend it had turned into a butterfly and flown away. The day Miss Brenda shared her awful secret, it was sort of a medium larva.

That January morning, I rode my bike to Miss Brenda's Baton Barn for my private lesson. The studio was empty, and being the only twirler in that chilly space with its twenty-foot ceiling made me feel like the last Popsicle in the box. As soon as my hands thawed and we got started, I asked Miss Brenda to help me with a new trick I had been working on. She grabbed my baton, and it seemed to spin around her neck all on its own. Miss Brenda had this flow when she touched the baton, and a far-off look, like she was the bride and it was the groom and they were in love.

"You're so smooth," I said.

"Been doing this thirty-five years," said Miss Brenda. "Twirl in my sleep."

I pictured her baton whapping the ceiling with each throw as she snoozed. "Someday, I want to get as good as you," I said. I put the baton under my chin and used my neck to twirl it around my shoulders.

"You're something special, kiddo," said Miss Brenda. "With your natural flexibility and practice ethic, the sky's the limit." She gestured skyward and we both looked up. The baton I had gotten stuck in the rafters last week stared back at us. "Well, maybe not the sky. But at least the ceiling," she added. She was quiet for a moment, and when she spoke again her voice sounded, I don't know, heavier. Miss Brenda said, "There's something I need to tell you." She grabbed my baton mid-twirl. "I'm not supposed to say anything for another week, but, dang it, Mindy, I've known you since you were tiny, even taught your mom. I've got to give you a heads-up." She looked like she would burst into tears.

"Are you okay?" I asked. She led me to her "office," a desk in a supply closet. I followed her past the photographs on the hallway walls, including the newest one of last year's Squadettes holding up a small trophy. They were standing in front of a fence, smiling cluelessly while behind each girl's head metal things poked out like alien antennas. Looking at the team pictures made me feel left out sometimes, but there were lots of photos of me holding the trophies I'd won for my solo routines.

"I don't know how to break this to you, kiddo," Miss Brenda said as I sat on a box in her office, "but here goes. I'm selling out. Got an offer from the Cluck and Shuck chicken corn soup franchise for the land, enough for me to buy a condo in Florida. Baton is a young gal's sport. I've got no regrets. But at fifty-eight, it's time to face facts. A girl's gotta look out for herself.

I'll take you twirlers to the Twirlcrazy Grand Championship in May, but after that I'm through."

It felt like I'd been whacked in the gut with a 7/16-inch Fluted Super Star. "But Miss Brenda, you're the only baton studio in town, and, even if you weren't, there's no way we could afford to pay someone else for my lessons."

"Sorry, kiddo. I wish it didn't have to be this way."

"This can't be happening to me. What will I do if you close?"

"You'll land on your feet somehow." Then she must have said a bunch of other stuff to try to make me feel better, but I wasn't listening because I was thinking about how my life had been completely ruined. "Until I make an announcement," said Miss Brenda, "this is just between you and me. Right?"

She winked, and I gave her one of those pretend smiles we use in competitions, but inside I was ticked. Miss Brenda was wrong about me. I wasn't one of those girls who could land on her feet. I was good at only three things: being tall, being tanned, and being a twirler. And let's face it, being tall and having free use of Mom's tanning bed weren't things I could really take credit for. Twirling wasn't just an activity I did for fun like some of the Squadettes, who also took horseback riding lessons and ballet classes. Twirling was all I had.

When I was twirling, nobody called me stupid, snickered behind my back, or told dumb-blond jokes that they changed to dumb brown-haired to fit me. When I did a perfect split-leap pullout, not a single person in the audience cared what I scored on a standardized test, or that I had failed math my first semester of eighth grade and might get held back.

If the Baton Barn closed, my competitive twirling days would be over, and I'd be just another one of the dumb kids. Life was so unfair. Why did I always get the short end of the baton?

3 Aphrodite Describes Meeting Mindy for the First Time

If you're skinny and flat, like me, here's a fun thing you can do. Stand in front of a full-length mirror. Turn your body sideways. Now stick out your tongue. Behold! You're a zipper. I felt chipper as a zipper the morning I got dressed for my first day of teaching at Carnegie Middle School.

I wore the gray suit I used for presentations at Harvard, but tucked a pink silk handkerchief way down low in the front pocket of the jacket where nobody but I could see it. Even though my professors at Harvard discouraged me from wearing pink because it was "too little-girly" and "suggested a failure to appreciate the importance of a professional appearance," it was still my favorite color.

How did I make the transition from brilliant math

prodigy and Harvard graduate student to thirteen-year-old middle school remedial math teacher, you might be asking? More about that later. Suffice it to say that after my new-teacher orientation, I sat at the desk in front of my eighth-grade classroom waiting for the students to trickle in. I couldn't remember if I had been in the same classroom when I had attended Carnegie Middle School as a student, since I had passed through so quickly. Boring describes that room: naked bulletin board, crooked rows of wooden student desks, and dingy white walls. My gray suit sure didn't help to pep things up, so I pulled up the pink handkerchief till it peeked out of my breast pocket.

I knew it might feel a bit awkward at first teaching students who were the same age as me. However, I was confident that my air of authority and superior mathematical skills would make it impossible for any of the thirteen-year-old students in my class to think of me in any way other than as the distinguished educator I intended to be.

A boy wandered in and came over to my desk, leaning in close. He had a chubby face, yellow teeth, and the worst breath I had ever smelled. "Why are you sitting there?" he asked. He punctuated his consonants with big bursts of air. "Park your butt in the back."